REVAMPED

ELISE ABRAM

ALSO BY ELISE ABRAM

"Tell me about your childhood," she said. She poised her pen above the paper, ready for note-taking.

"There's nothing to tell," I answered softly.

She chuckled quietly. "Surely, you must remember something."

I shook my head. There really was nothing to tell. It was as if I hadn't existed before three weeks ago. As if I were just newly born.

"Let's approach this from a different angle, shall we?" She looked at me and smiled. They'd assigned me the grandmotherly type, round and jolly with high, rosy, crab apple cheeks. She wore her hair curled tightly around the circumference of her face, newly-grown grey hugging her hairline like a tiara. "What's the very first memory you recall?"

I thought for a moment before answering so she'd get that my response was genuine. "Waking up. In the hospital. Before I came here." I closed my eyes and tried to go back to a time before that, but all was mist and fog.

"Okay." She made a note in my file. "Let's explore that memory.

"Close your eyes. Take a deep breath. Imagine you're there."

Visualization. We'd tried it before. Visualize your parents. Visualize the house you grew up in. Visualize your childhood friend. It hadn't worked then. I didn't know what made her think it would now, but I played along. I closed my eyes, took a deep, cleansing breath, and tried to remember the hospital into which I'd been reborn.

"It's cold. I'm shivering," I told her.

"Good," she said. "What colour is the room?"

"Light blue. The colour of a cloudy sky."

"Very good." I imagined the edges of her mouth turned up into a smile at my revelation. "Who's with you in the room?"

"I'm alone. There are magazines on the end table and a water pitcher on a tray on wheels over my bed near my knees."

I heard her clothes rustle; the sound of her nodding. "How did you get there?"

"I don't know."

"In the time before you were placed in the cold room—"

"There's nothing." I opened my eyes and frowned. "I don't exist before then." Shortly after I was reborn, I began to think of my life as being the sum of two wholes. I had come to think of my life before I existed as "The Before" and my life after rebirth as "The Now". The divisor between the two was some unknown devastating event, a huge caesura cleaving me—who I was, who I am, and who I will be—in two.

"Calm down, Janet," the doctor said. "Take another breath. A deep one. In through the nose to the diaphragm. Out through the mouth...good. And again..."

Janet isn't really my name. Technically, I guess I'm a Jane Doe, one of two brought to the hospital that night. Some nurse had the brilliant idea to name one of us Jane and the other Janet; I guess I pulled the short straw. I kind of liked it at the time, you know? Janet. It rhymed with planet which made me feel out of this world, extraordinary, rather than some less than ordinary blank slate, one with no identity or memory. If I had to be anybody, I suppose Janet Planet was infinitely better than blah old plain Jane Doe.

Dr. Putnum coached me through three more breaths and then said, "Good. I think we're done for the day." She smiled proudly, as if we'd actually accomplished something in the session. "We'll pick up with this again tomorrow."

She nodded, ignoring me in favour of her furious note-making as I left.

An orderly from my wing was waiting on the other side of the door to walk me to my room for nap time. Nap time! Like I really was newly born and in need of rest, when all I really wanted was to break free of my cage and soar. If I were ever to figure out who I was—who I really was—I was sure it was out there, in the real world, and not stagnating in a near-rubber room on the inside. Someone knew me out there. Someone out there would claim me and help me to reclaim myself.

The orderly left me alone. I went straight to the bathroom, dim with the light out, and examined my features in the mirror. I looked like me—at least, I thought I did. I couldn't be sure if it were a latent memory from The Before, or a new one, formulated in the more recent Now.

I fixated on the face staring back at me, hard, until my vision blurred and my features melded into the surrounding darkness.

Something was wrong. The face in the reflection was me, but not me. This must be the way it feels to look at oneself in the mirror after reconstructive surgery, I thought. That metaphor seemed to fit best.

I couldn't explain it any clearer than that my reflection was somehow off.

An hour later, it was time for Group. Dr. Putnum was there. So were about a half-dozen other people from my ward.

My ward was a wayward home for lost souls. My ward-mates, each of them secure in their own delusions, were even more lost than I. We had all somehow forgotten ourselves. Somewhere inside us all, we had erected a dam. Our psyches stood beside that dam, stubbornly plugging up the only method of egress with a finger. Two scenarios were inevitable: we would eventually pull the finger out and allow our true selves to leak through, or the hole would crack under pressure, slowly expanding until our psyches rushed back in the blink of an eye. Gone one moment, here the next; sudden realization. Either way, we would all eventually be damned to suffer with who we were until the end of our days.

On my ward was a girl who had cleaved herself in two— Emma, the Prim and Proper and Christina, the Promiscuous;

Edgar the Goth, who believed himself to be a vampire; Grace, who had been abused by her father and chose to slit her wrists rather than turn him in to the authorities; Ray, former crack addict and habitual runaway who was there to dry out and find God in the process (or so his parents hoped); and Milo, perpetual greaser who dressed and acted as if he was forever lost in the fifties.

Edgar had just finished his schpiel, the now tired story of how he craved blood and wished we would move Group to night, so he didn't have to duck and cover each time he passed a window. Dr. Putnum was in the process of ending Group when Milo raised his hand. "Dr. Putnum, we haven't heard from Janet today," he said earnestly.

"I have nothing to say," I responded, breaking my promise to ignore Milo's taunts.

"You never have anything to say," Edgar chimed in.

Grace began to sing softly to soothe herself. Others affirmed Edgar's sentiment.

"There's nothing to tell, okay?" I said, raising my voice.

"There's always something to tell," Edgar prodded.

"Not for me." I thought for a moment, willing something—anything—to come through. "There's nothing to tell because I don't remember anything," I told them whilst glaring at Edgar.

"Wow," Milo said, "that's a bitch." I almost believed the sentiment.

"Memories are a bitch," Christina said (at least, I think it was Christina). "If you asked me, Janet won the lottery. What I wouldn't give to wipe some of *my* memories clean."

There was momentary silence. Milo broke it when he said, "What lottery? Memories are who you are, man. I embrace my

9

past. If I had the chance to do it all again, I wouldn't change a thing."

"Surely, there must be *one* thing, Milo?" Dr. Putnum asked.

"What? No. No. No. No. You can't do that. We were talking about Janet," Milo said.

"We were. We *were* talking about Janet, and now we're talking about you."

"No. No, we're not."

"We *are*, Milo. You said you wouldn't change a thing if you had to do it all again. Don't you have any regrets?"

"I regret I didn't kiss Annabeth in tenth grade," Milo said, grinning.

"I had a dream last night," I told Dr. Putnum in Session. "About Milo." I hadn't planned to tell her about it, but since I was there and needed something to talk about, I kind of blurted it out.

Dr. Putnum shifted in her seat. "Go on," she said.

"I woke up. In my dream. And there he was. Lying on top of me." No, that wasn't right. There was no weight, and there had been space between us. "More like…floating above me. He said he wanted to tell me something.

"I propped myself up in bed so we'd be closer. He said he wanted to whisper it to me because he was in my room, and he wasn't supposed to be there.

"I remember thinking that I should be afraid and wondering how Milo had gotten into my room when they lock the rooms at night, and I was going to ask him, but then he smiled, and I felt like I knew him—"

"You *do* know him. From the Ward. From Group."

"No, not like that. I mean, I knew him…from before."

"Oh," Dr. Putnum said, exclamation fraught with realization.

"No!" I said, "God, no. Not like that. I mean, it felt like he had been in my life before. Like he was someone I could trust."

"Then what?"

"He smiled at me, and I forgot any doubts I might have had about him."

"You said he had something to tell you?"

I nodded. "So, I propped myself up in bed so we'd be closer, and so he could whisper whatever it was he wanted to say into my ear.

"Suddenly, his smile grew...I don't know...sinister, his eyes seemed to glow, like a cat's eyes will in the light, and he said, 'We are a lot more alike than you know, Prudence,' and then he was on top of me, and it was hard to breathe, and I woke up.

"I was shaking, drenched in sweat. I couldn't get the look he gave me out of my mind.

"'We are a lot more alike than you know.' What did he mean by that? And Prudence! He called me Prudence! Is that my name? Who the hell am I?"

Dr. Putnum managed to talk me down before dismissal from Session, reassuring me that my dream had been good. A revelation. A breakthrough. Dreams were like windows to the soul, she'd said. She'd smiled and went back to focus on her notes.

The orderly led me outside and deposited me on a bench in the garden to think.

Prudence.

The Beatles' song sprung to mind.

Spring was testing the waters to see if she was ready to jump in and breathe new life into the world. There were few clouds in the sky. Tufts of snow played chicken with the sunlight, daring each other to hold their ground. The snow would lose eventually, but not before a few more sallies against the sun.

I turned my face up to warm my cheeks in the sunlight, wondering when had been the last time I'd appreciated nature, the circle of life, the seasonal cycle of birth, death, and rebirth, when the orderly came to shoo me back inside for my nap.

Though I was tired, found I could not sleep no matter how I tried.

It was the sunlight. My mind kept returning to the sunlight and the warmth it had beamed onto my skin; my body craved it.

I stretched a blanket over the floor beneath the sole window in my room and lay on it, so I could once more feel the warmth on my skin. At last, I fell asleep.

When I aroused from sleep, it was to the sound of the orderly's gasp. I awoke to the scream of his voice as he hollered down the corridor for a medic. It seemed loud enough to wake the dead. I didn't understand what his problem was until I stood up and caught my reflection in the mirror through the bathroom doorway. My hand rose to my face and touched the tender skin it found there.

Burned. I'd been burned, and severely so. Dime-sized blisters covered my face and exposed forearms like a pox.

The medic rushed into the room. "Dear God," he said when he first saw me. "What did you do, Janet?" he asked, as if I'd burned myself intentionally.

"What do you mean, 'what have I done'? What's happening to me?"

Dear Prudence, I thought, and shuddered.

Dr. Putnum whirled into the room. "My God," she said. "What happened, Janet? Who did this to you?"

"Nothing," I said, fighting to catch my breath. "No one." I couldn't breathe. The room began to darken around me and then I fell.

I awoke in the infirmary, ointment slathered onto my cheeks and forehead, and I assumed, my forearms as well, though I couldn't tell as they were swathed in gauze.

"Second-degree burns," the medic said.

"What?" I answered, still groggy. My flesh burned. I longed for the cool, brisk breath of winter.

"How did this happen, Janet?"

"I don't know. I fell asleep in the sunlight, and the next thing I knew—"

The medic shook his head. "I have a hard time believing all this is from the sun. And through a closed window, no less."

"I'm telling you: I was asleep. I don't know what happened."

"Chalk it up to one of the mysteries that is Janet," he said. He deposited my chart at the foot of my bed and smiled before leaving.

Three days later, I marked the end of my two-week observation period. My burns were sufficiently healed that the medic was willing to sign my infirmary release papers. Dr. Putnum? Not so much. She pleaded I stay until I'd recovered more of my memories than an errant name. The thought of my following the hospital's geriatric schedule for even another day sealed the decision for me in the long run.

I left with little more than a bag containing the clothes that had been on my back when I'd arrived. The laundry hadn't been able to do much with my clothing, Dr. Putnum had explained. I opened the bag to see light copper-coloured stains on a pair of razored skinny jeans, and a mottled afterburn on a cream-coloured silk blouse that appeared to have been razored as well. Judging by the labels on the clothes and their style, I had money somewhere. Either that, or there was someone out there with money who had taken care of me.

Dr. Putnum sent me off with a sweater she'd bought me as a going away gift. The nursing staff presented me with a fashion cap and matching scarf and gloves. As I had no forwarding address, Dr. Putnum made arrangements for me to stay at a local shelter.

When the social worker came to get me, Dr. Putnum gave me her card. She urged me to call her if I needed anything, even a friendly shoulder to cry on. I left feeling apprehension about my decision to go for the first time since I'd made up my mind. I had no money, no purpose, and no people searching for me. I was, for all intents and purposes, alone in the world.

The night at the shelter was uncomfortable, to say the least. Women and children were warehoused in small rooms, many of them crying, even in their sleep. The social worker assigned me a cot, but I don't think I slept more than a wink or two before morning.

Breakfast was served cafeteria-style. I won't complain about the food—my last meal had been…I don't know when, and I was just thrilled to have something to stop my hunger from growing. Rather than engaging in polite conversation with the other women, I kept to myself and sat in a corner, contemplating my situation.

The shelter was a temporary solution to my problem. I'd left the hospital wearing blue surgical scrubs, but the social worker at the shelter had given me a pair of leggings and a t-shirt to wear. Aside from the stains—which looked suspiciously like dried blood, the clothes I'd been wearing when I'd arrived at the hospital had been ripped to shreds. I'd thrown them out before I'd left the hospital. Funny—I hadn't a scratch on me.

If it wasn't *my* blood on the clothes, then whose was it? Was it even possible for my clothes to have been shredded like that while still on my body and for me to have emerged unscathed?

While I sipped my orange juice, the social worker from the night before sat at the table opposite me. "Hey, Janet," she said. She dropped a folder she was carrying onto the table in front of her. The tab on the folder read "Janet Doe". It was mine. It measured my life in sheets of paper. Needless to say, it was pretty thin.

I smiled at her. "I'm sorry. Last night was..." I couldn't finish the sentence—I had no idea what the night before had been. "In all the...craziness, I'm afraid I didn't get your name."

"It's Persephone," she said, smiling. "Most people just call me Seph."

"That's an unusual name," I told her.

"The goddess of spring and daughter of Zeus and Demeter." She looked at me, gauging my reaction. "My mother was a Classical Studies major.

"Any memories yet?" she said without skipping a beat.

"Not even one."

"Well, good news on that front..." She opened the folder and handed me a small envelope.

"What's that?" I asked.

"The police gave it to me. They found it on a drunk they hauled in."

Inside the envelope were a few credit cards, a set of keys, and a driver's licence and hospital card belonging to Addison Haney with my picture on them. "This is me?" I asked. "I'm Addison?"

"Right you are."

I piled the items on top of the envelope and slid it back across the table to her. "That doesn't sound right," I said.

"Honey, pictures don't lie." She smiled at me, tight-lipped. "More good news: your car's in impound. You can pick it up any time."

All I could manage to say was "How? Where?"

"Well, they didn't tell me that, but I can take you there later. First order of business is to check out your digs to see if we can't jog any memories loose."

The address was to a condominium apartment near the waterfront. We went up to the penthouse and used the keys to let us in. No sooner had the door opened than an alarm sounded. As if on autopilot, I went to the alarm panel and typed in my PIN. I turned to Seph to see her mouth had dropped. I shrugged. "Muscle memory, I guess," I said, as baffled as she.

The condo had been tastefully decorated in blacks and greys with small bursts of colour—mostly red accents—on throw pillows and artwork.

"Anything?" Seph asked eagerly, almost as if she had a stake in my remembering. Maybe she got a bonus for every case put successfully to rest.

I shook my head and kept exploring. The kitchen had a white ceramic floor and backsplash and stainless steel appliances. The cabinets had glass panels in them, showcasing the bright red ceramic plates and mugs inside. Other than the china in the cabinet, there was no sign the kitchen had ever been used.

"I think the bedroom's this way," Seph told me, and I followed her, passing a guest bathroom on our way down the hall. The bedroom was just as sparse as the rest of the apartment—no personal touches anywhere. I went into the walk-in closet to see a beautiful wardrobe, most every piece—including the underwear sitting in a basket on a shelf—black.

"This can't be mine," I said. "I don't feel at home here." It was true—none of it seemed like me. Though I was sure I wouldn't mind black clothing, the loneliness that had drilled a hole in my heart of late told me I was more of a nester, that there should be something to indicate the place was mine. There should be pictures. Even if I were single and without children, there should be something—parents, siblings, friends?

"It's a lot to take in, I know," Seph said. She put a cold hand on the small of my back. "Head injuries are unpredictable. Maybe after you've spent some time—"

"You're leaving me?" My heart beat double-time. Small beads of sweat broke out on my upper lip at the realization.

"I have other cases to check on." She used the hand on my back to lead me down the corridor toward the front door. "I'll be by to see you tomorrow. My advice? Go out and familiarize yourself with the neighbourhood. See if you can't jog a few memories loose while you're at it."

That was when things got weird. She put the same cold hand on the back of my neck, took a step closer to me, and touched her forehead to mine, invading my personal space. Just when I thought she was about to lean in a little closer to kiss me, she pulled away and said, "You'll be fine."

She opened the door, stepped out into the hall, and turned to face me again. "Here's my card," she said, passing it to me. "If you need anything, anything at all, call me. I'm a bit of a night owl, so don't let the time of day stop you from calling."

Seph sighed and buried her hands deep inside her jacket pockets. "I'll be back tomorrow to get your car out of hock. Until then…" She waved and walked down the hallway toward the elevators, stopping halfway. "Lock up tight while I'm gone, okay?" she called.

I nodded, waited until the elevator doors closed behind her, and did exactly as she'd said.

I woke up early the next morning, found a thin, long-sleeved, black sweater, a powder blue tank, and a pair of dark jeggings in the bedroom closet. Most of "my" clothes were black; I'd have to remedy that situation as soon as I could. I was in the kitchen searching for coffee when Seph knocked on my door. When I didn't answer after the first knock, she called to me. "C'mon, Addie, open the door. We have things to do today."

At first, I ignored her. The only thing I needed from her was to take me to the impound lot to free my car. Other than that, I needed time to myself to get reacquainted with me.

When I didn't answer, her knocks grew more insistent, almost frantic. I was about to give in and answer when she stopped. No more than ten seconds later, the phone on my landline rang. Rather than answer it, I went directly to the door.

Seph gave a deep sigh of what sounded like relief when she saw me. "You're okay! I was beginning to worry." I'd say she left worry in the rear-view mirror a while ago and was bordering on downright distraught. No matter the sentiment, her reaction set off all sorts of warning bells in my mind. I chalked it up to the fact that she was the social worker assigned my case, and she was worried she'd lose her job if something happened to me.

"You ready to go?" she asked.

Seph was wearing a long-sleeved, full-length, form-fitting, black dress. "When you are, Morticia," I wanted to answer but suppressed the urge as being too familiar, given our relationship. I nodded instead. "I just need to grab my purse," I told her.

"Don't forget the hat," she said, pulling a very wide-brimmed, straw hat from seemingly out of nowhere and setting it on her head.

"I have one of those?"

"Oh, child—it's as if you were born yesterday." She practically pushed me out of the way to enter my apartment, started down the hallway toward my bedroom, paused midway, turned, and said, "I suppose you sort of were."

"Wait," I closed the front door and followed her down the hallway, "where are you going?"

She disappeared into my bedroom and came out seconds later with a black straw hat similar to hers, only mine had a white band at the base of the crown.

"Let's go," she said.

"How did you know—"

"I noticed it yesterday when we were checking the place out." She made a beeline for the front door. I seemed to have no choice but to follow her out.

Seph had parked in one of the disabled spots nearest the building's doors. I didn't question why a seemingly able-bodied, fit young woman would need to have a disabled pass. Her car was a black (no surprise there) Volkswagon bug with tinted windows. She got into the car, put a pair of rather large sunglasses on, and turned the key in the ignition.

The first item on our agenda was to rescue my car from impound. According to the key, I drove a Toyota. I hoped for a sporty model, was kind of disappointed when I saw it was a Corolla, but relieved to see it was a lovely cherry red with surprisingly dark, tinted windows. The jury was still out on my lifestyle. Either I was a high-end, colour-loathing fashionista, or I was an emo-Goth loner. The splash of colour on my car was a welcome step in the chic direction.

"Thanks for your help, Seph," I said, ready to drive off the lot.

"Not so fast, my dear." She put a hand on my arm. "We still have things to do."

"I think I can take care of things on my own from here."

"Nonsense."

"Really," I assured her, "I'll be fine."

"I'm afraid I can't let you go into the great wide open on your own just yet, my friend." I looked at her as if she might have something up her sleeve—her rather tight, black, long sleeve. When I didn't look away, she gave an exasperated sigh. "Number one in the social worker's rulebook: never leave a new charge to her own devices on day one, especially one with amnesia."

"You're making that up," I told her.

She held three fingers up on her right hand. "Scout's honour."

Though I doubted there was such a volume as the *Social Worker's Rulebook*, I gave her the benefit of the doubt and made a mental note to look it up later online, when I got home. Something was off about this Persephone. The card she'd given me had seemed legit, but then again, anyone can have a card printed with practically anything on it these days. She was another thing I'd have to remember to look up when I had the chance.

"Fine," I said with a great exhalation of air. "Where to next?"

"You lost your cell phone in whatever happened to you. We need to get you a new one."

"Maybe I should cancel my subscription instead." Seph looked at me weirdly. "I mean, I don't really have anyone I could call."

"You have me," she said. "Besides, it's good to have one in case of an emergency."

"Fat lot of good it did me the last time."

"Past history aside, every girl needs to have a cell phone. It could come in handy now that you're..." She stopped herself from finishing the sentence and opened the driver's side door of her car. "Do you remember where Yorkdale is?"

"Now that I'm what, Seph?" I wasn't about to let that statement go. "What's different about me now? Have the police figured out what happened to me?"

Seph looked at me as if deciding how much information she should spill. After a moment, she said, "You must be famished. Meet me at the Pick, and we'll have a bite." She smiled widely, shrugged, and climbed into her car.

I tried to follow her as closely as I could on the way to the restaurant, hoping I'd get some answers there.

The human brain is a funny thing. Parts of it can be destroyed without affecting personality or behaviour, but damage the wrong part of it, and the essence of who we are as people can forever vanish. Luckily, whatever happened to me had taken away my short-term memory, but left me with a quite extensive long-term one. For example, I remembered how to drive, but not the number on my licence plate. I remembered where Yorkdale was, but I hadn't remembered my address only two nights before.

Seph and I met again in line at the Pickle Barrel in Toronto's Yorkdale Shopping Centre. The restaurant itself was underground, done up in polished panelling, and surprisingly bright for what was essentially a basement. The maître d' led us to a table open at one end and encircled with a high-backed bench on all other sides in which we were guaranteed relative privacy.

"Seph, what did you mean—"

She held up a hand to silence me and handed me a menu. "Order first."

The menu was huge. Just looking at the pictures made my mouth water, and I realized I couldn't remember the last time I'd eaten. One thing was for sure: I was getting french fries.

"Are you sure?" Seph asked when I told her. I looked at her dumbly, not sure why she'd ask. "I mean, you look like the kind of girl who takes good care of her body, someone who might want to order something…I don't know—healthier?"

"Thanks for the advice, but I think what I've just been through—whatever it was—warrants some fries. *And* a burger. I think I'll have a burger, too."

The waitress came, and I ordered. I could've sworn Seph winced when I ordered the burger well-done. I wondered which set of rules in the *Social Worker's Handbook* governed controlling the food choices of one's charge. Hadn't I already said something seemed off about the woman?

Seph ordered liver and onions—nothing odd about that, right? To each her own comfort food, I guess.

"Can we talk, now?" I said once I was sure the waitress was out of earshot.

"Absolutely."

I opened my mouth to ask my burning question, but Seph said, "First we get you a phone, then food—even if there's stuff in your fridge, I'm sure it's spoiled by now," before I could get out word one.

"Next—"

"That's not what I meant."

"I know what you meant," she said quietly.

"Then why are you avoiding the question? What don't you want me to know?"

"The police haven't found anything," she said, shredding the corner of her napkin.

"What do you know that you're not telling me."

"Nothing," she began. "I don't—" She stopped herself when the waitress reappeared to deliver our drinks: a cola for me and a tomato juice for Seph. When the waitress had left, Seph continued, "I don't know what happened to you, dear."

I let out a chuckle. "I can't shake the feeling I know you from somewhere."

25

"You do," she said. My heart fluttered with excitement. "You know me from the hospital and the shelter, remember?"

My heart slowed and seemed to drop in my chest. "That's not what I meant, and I think you know that."

"Addie, sweetie, you suffered a traumatic brain injury. Your eggs are all scrambled—who knows what you meant."

I took a sip of my pop, and a thought occurred: "How did you know to call me Addie?"

Seph had raised her glass to take a sip, but she stopped midway at my question and set the glass back atop what was left of her frayed napkin. "I just assumed—"

"No, you didn't. It's almost like you knew."

"I could call you Addison if you prefer, but I believe in economy of words, and Addison's three syllables whereas Addie's only two."

She was right. Addie seemed the natural contraction of Addison. Then again, Addison as a name was in and of itself unusual, particularly for a woman, and Addie did sound a bit more feminine. "No, Addie's fine."

"Well, then, why all the hoopla?" She raised her glass once more and took a sip. "Honestly, girl, you *are* high maintenance, aren't you?"

"I wouldn't know," I told her.

"No, I suppose you wouldn't," she confirmed.

After eating lunch and procuring a replacement phone, Seph took me to the drugstore and convinced me to buy a bottle of iron pills, insisting it would help rid my brain of residual lethargy from the concussion causing my memory loss. I bought the pills to get her off my back and not because I believed them to be the magic cure-all for whatever ailed me.

Being with Seph was weird, to say the least. She was a close-talker—a little too close for all but my most intimate of partners, had I any. She was also too handsy for my liking. At one point, she grabbed for my hand, and I wondered if she had circulation problems—her hand was as cold and clammy as a dead fish, which creeped me out. I pulled my hand away, feigning an itch on my nose. Besides her proximity and hands-on approach, I didn't want to give her the wrong idea. As far as I knew, I didn't swing her way—correction: I wasn't sure which way I swung yet—but I didn't want to lead her on. I didn't want to be with anyone at that particular juncture in time, male or female. What I really needed was some alone time to reacquaint myself with me.

I managed to shake Seph in the parking lot, pretending to slip into my car as I watched her drive away. On first glance, my wardrobe had been too monochromatic for my liking. However it had become that way, it was time to add a pop or two of colour, so I went back into the mall.

A few pairs of jeans and brightly-coloured t-shirts and blouses later, I was back at my car where I tossed my bags into the backseat. It seemed too hot out for wearing black, let alone wearing a long-sleeved sweater, no matter how thin, so I pulled it off. I scratched an itch at the back of my neck, and it occurred to me I'd forgotten my hat in the mall. For a brief moment, I toyed with the idea of going back for it, but the hat hadn't seemed my style—whatever that was—from the moment I'd put it on, and I decided to leave it; good riddance to bad rubbish, as far as I was concerned.

I threw the sweater into the backseat with my bags, got into my car, and began the trek home. Though I remembered how to turn the air conditioning on—muscle memory again—I decided to open the window and get a bit of fresh air. I turned the radio on. It was set to CBC talk radio—I guess it would do until I figured out my taste in music—and rested my elbow on the edge of the open window.

It wasn't long before the sun's rays began to burn. Warm and welcome at first, it quickly deepened to an itch and then to a burn, and I pulled my arm in and closed the window. By the time I'd stopped at the next light, my forearm was bright, angry, and red enough to practically disappear when held up against my car's paint job. The same thing had happened back at the hospital after I'd fallen asleep beneath the open window.

Once was a chance happening; twice was a habit. It was time I took it to a medical doctor, but which one? I drove past a big-box grocery store advertising an in-store pharmacy and walk-in clinic and pulled into the lot.

"Of course, I can't be sure," the doctor said after examining me, "but the rapid onset of tissue damage suggests photosensitivity polymorphous light eruption—or PLME—in particular. It could also be a condition known as solar urticaria, though both that and PLME usually manifest in one's young adult life, and you say you've only experienced this once before, and recently, at that."

"That's just it, Doc: I don't know how many times I've experienced this before."

He looked at me from under his extremely large brow ridge and bushy, grey eyebrows as if he'd misunderstood what I'd said, so I clarified. "I've recently suffered a brain injury. I woke up in the hospital afterward with no recollection of my life either before or during the accident." I let out a guffaw. "I don't even know if I had an accident, so when you ask if I've experienced this before, outside of once in the hospital and now, I couldn't tell you, but it feels as if I'm being burned alive, here."

"Hmm." He turned to remove his gloves and wash his hands in the sink at the corner of the exam room, "That's…unusual, to say the least."

I nodded. "Tell me about it."

He dried his hands, sat down at his computer, typed a bit, then swiveled his chair so he could speak with me face-to-face.

"Either way, the rash should fade within a few hours to a few days, depending on the root cause."

"A few days?" I said, trying not to whine.

"In the meantime, try cold-compresses, an over-the-counter antihistamine, and a cortisone cream. If that doesn't work, see your GP for a cortical steroid. In cases like this, it's better to be proactive rather than reactive. Wear long sleeves in sunlight, a wide-brimmed hat, and don't forget the sunscreen—I'd recommend something with a thirty SPF."

I thanked the doctor, wondering if I even had a GP to see, and purchased the remedies he'd suggested. While I was there, I did a quick shopping list, buying some cold cuts, bread, eggs, milk, yogurt, and Chicago-style popcorn. I picked up other groceries on a whim as I passed, hoping muscle memory was winning out again, and that I wouldn't suffer buyer's remorse for any of my purchases.

Carrying the bags of groceries up to my condo was awkward. I'd have to search my unit for a bundle buggy and buy one for the next time if I came up empty. I dropped the bags just inside my door, slid the locks into place, and made two trips to the kitchen to unload, shocked beyond belief when I opened the fridge.

Other than a few trays of ice cubes in the freezer and some frost, the fridge was near barren, save a pitcher of what looked like iced coffee and another that looked like iced tea. Besides that, the middle shelf was caked in a thin layer of what looked like spilled strawberry jam. I wondered if Seph had emptied my fridge of all perishables before giving back my keys. I didn't know whether to be grateful or wigged-out at the thought of her—a complete stranger—being in my apartment before I had been…or rather, before post-trauma me had been. Even if she was a social worker, even if she'd meant well, Seph had overstepped.

I reminded myself that I didn't know if it had been Seph in the first place. Maybe I'd done it *before* my accident.

That didn't make sense. Why would I have emptied my refrigerator of every last morsel of food?

Maybe there'd been a power outage and everything had spoiled.

It made sense. I resolved to check the Internet to see if there had, in fact, been a recent power outage in my neck of the woods, as soon as I was able to locate the whereabouts of my computer, if I had one.

I reminded myself that even if I didn't have a computer, which would be unusual in today's day and age, I had a data plan on my newly-minted phone and could look it up there.

Was the absence of a computer as unusual as the absence of food in my fridge—I checked the cupboards above the counter—and pantry, or even more so?

My first impulse was to ask Seph. I wondered—and not for the first time—if our relationship hadn't pre-dated my accident. What if I'd been a battered woman and my partner had beaten the concussion into me? What if the reason my apartment was near-barren was that it wasn't really mine, but a government safe house of some kind?

Seph had seemed surprisingly forward with me. What if she had been my abusive partner, and this was all a ruse designed to distract me from that fact?

I told myself I was overreacting. For some reason, the words "Occam's razor" popped to mind, that the simplest solution to a problem was usually the correct one. In this case, the fact that I'd been hurt in an as of yet determined accident, that Seph was my social worker, that I'd emptied my own fridge after a power-outage had spoiled its contents, and that I'd always had this photosensitivity, seemed to be the most plausible. I tried to convince myself of the merit of the assertion as I put the groceries away.

Who was Addison Haney? It was a question I was determined to answer, and as soon as possible. So far, my condo hadn't yielded any clues. To say I'd lived a spartan life was an understatement, judging by the pristine condition of my abode. I searched high and low but couldn't find a computer or a television, which was weird. There were no books, either—what did I do for entertainment?

Besides the pitchers of coffee and tea and the red china in the cupboards, the kitchen was barren. The living room wasn't much help, either. The bathroom had the usual toiletries: toothbrush and toothpaste; hand soap, moisturizer, and facial cleanser on the vanity; body puff, conditioner and hair and body shampoo in the tub. I appeared to have had good hygiene, but what told me more about my situation was what was absent. There was nothing in the mirrored, wall-mounted cabinet—no medication, either prescribed or over the counter, no ointments, and no bandages, either. There was no razor and no shaving cream. Apparently, I was in perfect health, never felt under the weather, and had a naturally hairless body.

Under the sink were spare rolls of toilet paper, boxes of Kleenex, and cleaning supplies for the kitchen and bathroom. There was also a small, mesh basket with an assortment of makeup, straightening and curling irons, and soft rollers. Female sanitary products were noticeably absent. So, I liked to clean, but I didn't have a monthly cycle. Maybe I'd simply run out of supplies, as far as Occam's razor was concerned.

On to the bedroom: king-sized bed, dresser with vanity, tall bureau, nightstands without drawers or cupboards. The dresser had drawers for underwear, socks, and other sundry items, but no papers, no receipts, no mad-money stash, and no pictures. Ditto for the bureau; I was batting zero.

The walk-in closet had shelves for delicate sweaters (most of them black). Hanging were pants, dress shirts, and dresses (most of them black). There were a number of wide-brimmed hats (either straw or felt, most of them black) on the shelf above the hanger rack. A shoe rack ran the perimeter of the closet under the clothes, housing almost every style of shoe you could think of (most of them black, too). A few of them had red soles, which told me I had money somewhere.

Having found no personal effects in my closet, I went back to the bedroom and flopped onto the bed to process. No matter how many ways I stacked the evidence, there was something eerie about the place. I was either some kind of extra-human oddity in that I had no personal effects and no sense of nostalgia, or the place truly wasn't mine.

The clock on the end table told me it was still within business hours. I decided the next step was to contact the condo's business office to find out who owned the place.

After an interminable wait while the office clerk disposed of the previous tenant, I took a seat at her desk. Before I could say word one, she said, "How are you doing today, Miss Haney?"

I felt my face drop. "You know me?"

"Of course." She surveyed my expression. "Are you okay, Miss Haney?"

"The jury's still out on that one," I said, forcing a smile.

She took a beat. "I don't understand."

"I appear to have had an accident. I say, 'appear', because I don't remember it. I don't remember much of anything, actually. I found my way home because the police recovered my ID, but I don't know much of anything else."

"Oh, dear. If there's anything I can do—"

A lightbulb went on somewhere in the recesses of my empty psyche. "Would you happen to have a file on me somewhere? If I could see anything—witness signatures on the title, cancelled cheques…anything—it might help to jog a few nuts loose."

"Of course," she said. She smiled, but it was kind of peculiar, like she didn't want to anger me lest I turn on her.

"Tell me something," I said as she went to check the filing cabinet in the corner, "do I have a reputation for having a hair-trigger?"

She gasped. "I'm not sure what you mean."

"Have you ever known me to have a temper?"

"Ah," she said, pulling a cream-coloured file from the drawer. "Here it is." She sat back down at her desk and handed me the folder, side-stepping my question entirely—chalk that up to an answer in the affirmative.

Funny—I didn't feel like I had a quick temper, which only went to show I still had much to learn, even if it was about myself.

According to the dossier they'd compiled on me, I paid my condo fees regularly and on time with post-dated cheques drawn from a CIBC branch down the street a bit. It was no surprise to find the witness on my condo agreement had been one Persephone Underwood.

I took my phone from my back pocket. "May I?"

"By all means," the clerk said.

I took pictures of the condo agreement and one of the cancelled cheques so I'd have my account number and branch address, closed the folder, handed it back to her, and said, "Thanks."

"Anytime, Miss Haney." She took the folder from me and set it in a mesh basket at the corner of her desk. "Is there anything else I can help you with?"

"What can you tell me about what's not in the folder?"

She gave a breathy titter. "I don't understand."

"Tell me what you know that you haven't written down. Have there been any complaints about me by the tenants? Has my unit ever flooded? Have I made any unusual demands of you or the superintendent?"

The clerk looked worried, and I began to wonder if she'd picked up the crazy card I'd played. "Not to my recollection."

"What about the super? How can I contact him?"

"Um, he's a she," the clerk said, "and here's her card."

I thanked her and said, "I'd appreciate it if you kept this conversation on the down-low. Please don't tell anyone, even Seph—"

"I'm sorry to hear that."

"Hear what?"

"That you and Miss Underwood are on the outs."

I smirked. "On the outs?"

"You made such a...lovely couple."

Something about the way she'd paused before saying lovely convinced me there was some sort of verbal irony at play. "Seph's my social worker."

"Oh!" She looked into her lap and blushed. "I'm sorry. I wasn't aware."

How *could* she have been when I didn't even know Seph before she was assigned my case?

"Okay," I said. "Thank you for the information." I stood up. "It's been...weird." I winked and nodded simultaneously and left the office.

In the corridor, I unlocked my phone and took a closer look at the condo agreement. Addison Haney was listed as the owner. No doubt about it, the condo was mine, lock, stock, and empty barrel. The other thing I needed to see was Seph's signature. If she'd signed as a witness, there'd also be a signing date.

I scrolled down to her signature and zoomed in on the date to find the contract had been signed two years ago.

Seph had been lying to me. If she wasn't my government-assigned social worker, then who was she?

The clerk seemed to think she was my partner. Were Seph and I an item? If so, why hadn't she told me?

Maybe she was waiting for my memories to return. Maybe she'd figured it was better for me to remember on my own than to force the situation.

A sudden wave of guilt washed over me—I'd been so wrapped up in my own drama, I hadn't thought of what Seph might be going through.

Something was rotten in the state of Denmark. If Seph was my partner, where were her possessions in the condo? Where were her clothes? Even if we didn't live together, shouldn't she at least have a drawer for her stuff?

It occurred to me that I couldn't even remember my name a few days ago—how would I know the difference between my underwear drawer and Seph's?

If Seph and I *had* been involved, shouldn't there have been at least two toothbrushes on the bathroom vanity? Shouldn't there have been two buff puffs, a loofah, something to indicate someone besides me slept there regularly?

My eyes watered with frustration. There was something seedy about the whole situation, and my insides burned to discover what it was, and now.

A voice inside my head told me Seph had somehow orchestrated the whole memory-wipe scenario, that she'd cleared my house of anything that might have jogged my memory to keep me in limbo about my past. The question was: why?

Let's say we *had* been regularly sucking face—why would she want to keep that a secret? If she kept me in the dark about my past, wasn't she also keeping *us* apart? Shouldn't she be showering me with *memento moris* so we could be together again that much sooner? Something about my current circumstance just didn't add up.

There was one last piece of real estate I had yet to ransack for clues, and that was my car, which had been locked up in impound since whatever it was had gone down. No way Seph could have gotten to its contents.

Down in the parking garage, I checked the trunk, first, but outside of a few reusable shopping bags and a small, six-pack-sized Thermos cooler box, there was nothing. The back and front seats were clean, too.

I got into the car and checked the glove compartment. Inside was a folder containing the car's manual, insurance and ownership, a bottle of hand sanitizer, and a few pocket-sized tissue packages.

There was a centre console between the driver's and passenger's seats. Inside the top tray were a quarter, a loonie, and a package of spearmint gum. I popped a stick of gum into my mouth, crumpled the wrapper and dropped it into the cup holder. The bottom tray of the console was filled with gas receipts. It looked as if I'd kept every single receipt for every single tank of gas I'd bought since I'd had the car.

I stuck my hand into the console and brought out a fistful of receipts and a book of matches. It was odder than odd because as far as I knew, I didn't smoke. If I'd smoked prior to my accident, surely I'd have had a craving by now or smelled it in my car, on my clothes, or in my condo, at the very least.

The matches had come from a place called Stoker's with a downtown address. When I looked the establishment up on my phone, I learned it was an after-hours club where it was the fashion for patrons to wear black while listening to the latest indie music.

Next stop on my magical mystery tour: Stoker's.

I put on a pair of black, twill, skinny pants with too many holes for my liking, a black, sleeveless t-shirt, and gladiator sandals I found in the closet and went to Stoker's. Seph called while I was putting my makeup on and texted as I was packing my purse, an over-the-shoulder, black, leather, mini-messenger bag. I ignored both of them. When I checked myself out in the mirror after having spent quite a bit of time straightening my hair—it was really long, and there was a lot of it—I was starting to feel more like myself, whatever that was. I found a stick of crimson lipstick—very high-end—in the basket of cosmetics, put some on, and stuck it in my purse for later touch-ups.

It was after midnight by the time I arrived at Stoker's. The doorman took a look at me, sneered, and moved aside to let me in.

The walls of the club had been painted black. Lighting was dark, save the starbursts on the walls and ceiling where the light reflected from hanging disco balls. I made my way through the crowd to the bar. When the bartender saw me, he said, "The usual?"

I wondered what that was. "Why not?" I told him. He turned his back and grabbed a martini glass.

"Hey, Pru," a tall, blond male with long, curly hair said. He reminded me of a less-buff Fabio.

The bartender slid my drink onto the bar, and it dawned on me that Fabio had called me Pru.

"Excuse me," I said, trying to maneuver away from Fabio and toward the bar, but he was standing just so damn close.

"How much do I owe you?" I asked the bartender.

"You know your money's no good here," he said, which frightened me a little. Maybe I didn't belong there. Maybe I was about to be thrown out.

Chill, Addie—if that were the case, he never would have served you.

He might if it were a diversion until the bouncer came.

I resolved to tread lightly until I had the lay of the land.

"Piers would literally kill me if I didn't treat you right." He smiled. "Enjoy," he said, and he went back to his other customers.

Whoever this Piers was, surely he wouldn't have *literally* killed him. People use the word literal in the figurative sense all the time, don't they?

"Give me a hug, love," Fabio said. He put a hand on my shoulder and spun me around to face him. Before I knew it, he'd enveloped me in a tight bear hug with my face smooshed against his rock-hard abs.

"I'm sorry," I said, wedging my hands into the crook of his elbows and pressing as a signal I wanted him to release his grip on me. "Do I know you?"

He let go of me, said something that sounded like "Ehh," smiled, and pointed his hand at me with the fingers shaped like a gun. "Good one." What Fabio had in brawn seemed to balance out with his lack of cool.

"We were getting a bit worried. You haven't been by in a while," he said.

"I've been...busy."

Fabio winked. "Right." He'd stretched out the "i" and winked, insinuating that whatever I was doing had been sexual in nature.

"You know me, right?" I asked.

"You're joking."

I looked at him for a moment. He thought I was this Pru person, whoever she was, and I wasn't about to correct him. The name struck a chord somewhere in my disconnected psyche. I'd heard it before; I was sure of it. The question was: where had I heard it and exactly which chord had it struck?

"Do you know Piers?"

"Of course, I know Piers. Everybody knows Piers."

"Is he here tonight?"

"Piers is here most every night," Fabio said.

"Take me to him."

Fabio made a small flourish with his hand and gave a slight bow—given the space between us, there was little room to do much more. "Your wish is my command," he said with a flip of his mane.

All sorts of warning bells went off in my mind: the bartender had been afraid of crossing Piers, be it literally or figuratively; Piers and I obviously had some kind of connection, or he wouldn't have arranged for my standing bar tab; and he was popular—everybody knew and respected him. Piers was either one hell of a stand-up guy to have garnered that kind or respect, or he was a total bad-ass. The rational half of my scrambled brain told me to leave, that this Piers guy was bad news, and I didn't want to get messed up with him; the lethe-enchanted half of my brain told me it was too late to give up. It also seemed confident that Piers was the key to my identity.

I took a sip of my drink. If I had to guess, I'd say it tasted of vodka, raspberries, blood oranges, and heaven. I signalled the bartender.

"Something wrong with your drink?" he asked, looking worried.

"What do you call this?"

"It's a Bloody Berry Martini. Virgin, just like Piers asked."

I took another sip of my drink to discover it was more slutty than virginal. Before I could take another taste to confirm, Fabio had taken my hand and was leading me around the dance floor, weaving between small, round tables and couples who had decided to engage in foreplay without the need of a room. "Watch your step," Fabio told me. I looked down to see two people—or maybe it was three—writhing on the floor. It looked as if they'd finished the foreplay but still hadn't thought to get a room. What was this place?

At the far side of the club, a number of beautiful men and women were sitting on a banquette behind a short, round, coffee table. "There he is," Fabio said. "Don't do anything I wouldn't do." He let go of my hand and disappeared back into the crowd before I could ask which of the men on the banquette was Piers.

Turns out, I didn't have to wait long to find out. The man at the centre of the banquette locked his striking green eyes with mine, stood up, and came toward me. He was wearing a black suit jacket and pants with a white, form-fitting dress shirt, open at the neck. When he was close enough to touch, he reached for my hands. I held the martini glass up in my left hand and gave him my right. "Prudence," he said, checking me out.

"Piers?" I said.

"You went for a casual look tonight—I like it." He pulled me close to him, let go of my hand, cupped my face, and gave me a long, deep kiss that melted my insides.

I wasn't in the habit of kissing strangers—at least, I didn't think I was—but there was nothing strange about that kiss. It felt like coming home, I'm not going to lie.

He pulled back to break the kiss, then leaned in again and whispered in my ear, "I know what you did, and I forgive you."

Piers pulled back again and looked at me with mesmerizing green eyes. His skin was light, though it was obvious one of his parents had been considerably darker. His hair was curly, shorn short on top, and buzzed on the sides. A few days' bristly stubble covered his cheeks.

"What did you say?" I asked. "What did I do?"

His smile didn't reach his eyes. "Not here. It is not safe." His smile broadened. "Come. Spend some time with me. It has been a while."

"I'm sorry…do I know you?" I said.

"Intimately." His reply sent chills down my spine.

Piers took my hand and tugged. "Come," he said, once more. He led me to the banquette against the wall, stopping in front of the middle seats. "Move," he told the people sitting there, and they parted like the Red Sea to give us space.

I heard someone sniff as if drawing in the aroma of a fine wine. When I turned, a middle-aged-man was smiling at me. "You smell delectable," he told me."

"Uh…thank you?" I said.

"Easy, Percival. She is still mine," Piers practically hissed.

"Sorry, Piers." The man looked at the floor. "I didn't mean anything by it. It's just…her perfume—it's alluring."

"If you cannot control yourself, Percival, you must leave Stoker's, never to return."

"I am sorry, Piers. It will not happen again."

"It had better not," Piers said.

I looked at him, and his face turned from icy serious to warm and smiley as if someone had flipped a switch. "It is nothing to worry about," Piers said. He put his arm around my shoulders and pulled me closer to him. When he leaned back into the plush banquette, he took me with him.

Though I still had no idea who this Piers was, I got the impression we'd been a couple and that we'd frequented the bar. He'd threatened Percival with banishment if he didn't behave, which meant he was either the owner of the place or some big mucky-muck in an interior turf claim. Regardless, I'd learned Piers had power—over the patrons and over me.

My cell phone buzzed, vibrating against my leg through the leather of my purse.

Seph—who else could it be?

I wondered at the dynamics between Seph and Piers. Had I been involved in a love triangle? Did Seph know Piers and vice versa? The question of what Piers had said he'd known I'd done lit a flame in the pit of my stomach.

His exact words had been: "I know what you did, and I forgive you."

What, exactly had I done?

That he'd forgiven me told me I'd hurt him in some way, betrayed him.

I thought of the bartender saying, "Piers would literally kill me if I didn't treat you right," and the command in Piers' voice when he'd threatened Percival's banishment—had he forgiven me because he loved me, or because he didn't want to exact consequence and hurt me back?

The DJ played a slow song. Piers removed his arm from my shoulders and stood in a quick, fluid movement. "Shall we?" he said, holding a hand out to me.

What I really wanted to do was leave. I wasn't sure if Piers was safe, scary, or a little bit of both. One thing I knew for sure, I was drawn to him as I had never been drawn to another person before; I'd like to think that if I'd ever been that far under another person's spell, I'd have remembered the feeling.

"Uh…okay," I said, and I let him lead me onto the dance floor.

People gave us wide berth to find a place that suited us—or maybe they were giving *Piers* wide berth to find a place that suited *him*. At any rate, when he was happy with our location on the dance floor, he pulled me toward him, wrapped his arms around my waist, and moved me even closer. I tried to look up into his eyes, but he put his chin near my shoulder and whispered, "It is safe to talk here."

I nodded.

"What have you done?"

"I thought you said you knew," I told him, unsure if I was being dumbly coy and flirtatious or keeping my cards smartly close to my vest.

"I know what you did, I just do not know how."

"If you know what, maybe you could fill me in?"

He pulled away from my shoulder to look me in the face. His eyes were hypnotizing. His lips formed a perfect, luscious cupid's bow. The desire to kiss them again was near overwhelming. "You do not remember?"

I shook my head.

"That is quite the side-effect," he said with a smile.

I gauged the situation—his reaction to me, my autonomic reaction to him, and the fact that he'd forgiven me—and decided it was safe to let my furious flag fly. "So glad you're amused with my suffering."

"Quite the opposite, my love." He tightened his grip on me and re-positioned his chin on my shoulder. "I asked you not to do it, but you disobeyed my wishes."

Hold on a second—*I* had disobeyed *him*? Who, exactly, was he to me? I'd surmised Piers had power, but what kind of power did he think he had over *me*?

"And those wishes were?"

The slow song ended, and a crazy punk song with lots of screaming and a strong beat took hold of the dance crowd. Those who responded to the soundtrack of the wild rumpus slammed into us, willy-nilly. "Not here," Piers screamed over the noise. "Not now."

He took my hand and tried to lead me off the dance floor, but I dug my heels in. "When?"

His lips formed a wicked grin. "All in good time, my pretty," he said, his eyes piercing mine."All in good time."

It was near four o'clock in the morning when Piers said, "The sun will be up soon. It is time to go." He helped me out of the deep, low banquette, bent his elbow, and hooked my arm in his.

Percival stood with us, taking a step in front of me to block my way. "Goodnight, my precious," he said.

Piers was between us in the blink of an eye. "Think hard and wise on what I have said, Percival. She is *mine*."

"I…I know," Percival said, cowed.

"Be certain, Percival. If you overstep again, I will make the choice for you."

"Yes, Piers," Percival lowered his eyes and took a step back.

Piers sidestepped the near-grovelling man, bent his arm again, and placed mine in the crook of his once more.

Outside of the club, Piers took me in his embrace and kissed me, long and passionately. It weakened my knees and took my breath away, and I was content to let him, happy to die in his arms at that very moment. Death by Piers—what a thought.

He broke the kiss and let his arms fall from my back.

"Is now a good time?" I asked.

"For what, my dear?"

"To discuss what I did that has you so riled."

Piers looked up to the still dark sky. "It is early. I should be getting home."

"But if it's early, there's still time to talk."

"Not here," he repeated. "Not now."

"So you've said."

"Let the past stay in the past, my dear. You came back to me, that is all that matters."

"I came to Stoker's because I found a matchbook in my car. Fabio found me, and he brought me to you."

"Fabio?"

I remembered having dubbed him Fabio because he'd reminded me of the model, and that I hadn't gotten his real name.

"I do not know this…Fabio."

"That's not my point—"

"Did he harm you?"

Outside of compressing my cheek against his monumental pecs...

I shook my head. "My point is: I didn't come back to you. I was trying to figure out who I was before…whatever, and the clues led me to you."

Piers grabbed me and pulled me close to him, wrapping me in his embrace. "The streets are dangerous, especially now. You must take care."

"Yeah," I said, having decided that Piers wasn't going to give me any answers in the near future, if ever. "I'll do that."

He walked me to my car, gave me a brief kiss on the cheek, and closed the driver's door once I'd buckled up. As I drove off, I saw him wave to me in my rear-view mirror.

I'd barely fallen asleep when there was a knock on my door. The bedside clock read 7:23 a.m. The pounding stopped for a moment, and I heard Seph call, "Addie? Are you in there?" This was followed by more pounding, then, "Addison Haney, you open this door this instant, or I'm coming in." I wondered how long before my neighbours either called the cops and/or filed a formal noise complaint with management.

"It's barely seven," I said, opening the door.

"Are you crazy?" Seph said, storming in.

"*Mi casa es su casa,*" I mumbled, but I don't think she heard. I also didn't think I spoke Spanish, but it was the first phrase to come to mind, and it seemed to fit.

Seph stopped in the approximate centre of my living room and wheeled around to face me. "You went to Stoker's last night?"

I turned to face her and pushed the door closed behind me. "Good news travels fast, I see."

"Are you crazy?" she asked again, her arms crossed over her chest.

"That *is* the general consensus," I said, trying to be sarcastic.

Seph dropped her arms to her sides and rushed me. "I was worried." She enveloped me in a tight hug. The brim of her hat scratched my forehead and fell to the floor. When she broke the hug, she took my face in her cold hands, much the same way Piers had the night before—come to think of it, his hands had been a little on the clammy side as well—and said, "Stoker's is dangerous. Especially now. Especially for you."

I reached up, grabbed her wrists, and pulled her hands away from my face. "Okay, well, I just went to bed a few hours ago, and I'm exhausted. I need coffee." Seph allowed me to sidestep her, and I headed for the kitchen.

"It won't help."

Her statement stopped me dead in my tracks, and I whirled around to give her a look.

"You only have decaf."

I opened my eyes wider as if to question the statement.

"Caffeine intensifies your cravings, so you switched over a while ago."

"Pop?"

"Uh-uh. You've cut back on sugar, too."

"I know I have fruit," I said, continuing on to the kitchen. When I'd gone shopping the day before, I bought a number of bananas. They were the sweetest things I could think of at the moment, so I broke one from the bunch, peeled it, and took a bite.

"You don't like bananas," she informed me. "You don't mind the flavour, but you find the texture off-putting."

I sat at the kitchen table. Though I hated to admit it, she was right. I found the sweetness cloying and the texture mushy. I swallowed before I could gag, lest I prove her right. When I was sure it would stay down, I challenged her know-it-all attitude with a grin.

"You're my social worker, right?" I asked.

"Assigned by Ontario's Ministry of Community and Social Services." She sounded proud.

"How many other cases do you have?"

She flashed me a thin-lipped smile. "I'm not at liberty to discuss my clients with other clients, Ad."

"Fair enough." I looked at the banana in my hand and paused before taking another bite. Damned if I wasn't going to finish it to spite the walking, talking, Encyclopedia of Addison Haney sitting in front of me. "Then tell me this: how do you know so much about me? I mean, how much you know— personal things like the caffeine and the banana—they make you seem more stalkerish than social."

"There's a file on you—"

"That lists my food preferences when I don't even know them myself? I couldn't have possibly been on the Ministry's radar until my incident—unless…was I? On the Ministry's radar?" My psyche felt intact. If someone had been beating or otherwise abusing me, I'd have known, wouldn't I? I mean, abuse takes its toll on a person—wouldn't I be cowering in fear under my blankets rather than venturing out into the great wide unknown like I had?

Unless I'd been the perpetrator.

Hadn't the bartender said Piers insisted he serve me virgin cocktails only? Maybe I was a recovering addict or alcoholic. Then again, if that were true, wouldn't I have consumed more than one of those...what had the bartender called it? Wouldn't I have consumed more than one of those bloodberry martinis in the hours I'd spent at Stoker's if that were the case?

Seph smiled. She reached across the table, took my hand, and squeezed in an effort to calm me. "You don't remember?"

"Remember what?"

"You weren't on our radar before your accident; you told me those things in the hospital when I took your medical history." She took a beat. "I'm not surprised you don't remember. You were in and out quite a bit in the beginning."

It sounded plausible. Still...

"So, we didn't know each other before my accident?"

"No, siree, bub."

"Huh," I said.

"What?"

"Nothing."

"It's obviously something, or you wouldn't have responded that way."

I shook my head, put the banana on the table, and let go of her hand. "I was just sure we'd known each other before. I've felt this...connection to you ever since we've met." It was a lie, designed to trump her lies and gain some intel on who she was and how she played into my current life situation.

"I'm so glad you said that." Her voice came out in a rush. "I've felt the same connection. I hope we can continue to be friends, even after your case times out."

Point: Seph.

"Why were you so upset about Stoker's?"

She leaned back in her chair and shook her head. "You're all right, that's the main thing. Stoker's doesn't matter anymore. Just…promise me you won't go there on your own again."

I mulled her request over in my head for a moment; I would do no such thing.

"I met Piers," I told her.

"I heard." She leaned forward and took both of my hands in hers. "Addison, you must promise to stay as far away from that man as possible. He's trouble. He's dangerous—"

"He seemed to think I somehow betrayed him. That's not something I might have told you about in the hospital when I was in and out, was it?"

Seph pressed her lips together and shook her head again. "Nope. This is the first I'm hearing about it." She leaned closer still. "What else did he say?"

"Nothing. I mean, he said he forgave me, but I got the feeling he was more of the strong, silent type, you know?"

"I know. Look, Addie, *you* weren't on our radar before, but Piers was. You need to stay away from him. Stay away from Stoker's, in fact, and anybody associated with it."

I nodded. Something didn't add up about Seph; never had. It was like she'd edited the important things I needed to know from her story. I needed to get rid of her and do some research in an attempt to gain back some of the information Seph had redacted.

"Look, Seph," I told her, "it was a late night last night, and I really need to get a bit of shut-eye. A shower might also be a good idea. Can I get in touch with you later?"

"I totally understand." She stood, walked to the front door, and reached for the doorknob, but then she let her hand drop. "I'm just glad you're safe." She turned to hug me.

I locked the door behind Seph, went back to my bedroom to get my phone, opened the browser, and typed "Persephone Seph Underwood" into the search bar. There were a number of hits for Joseph—who also went by the name of Seph—but none for Persephone. After the Facebook and LinkedIn listings, there were a few links for a number of people (and cats) named Persephone, pages with the names Persephone and Underwood on them, but not in direct association, and a number on Persephone, goddess of the underworld.

About ten pages deep into the search, I found a registry for an old, North Toronto church that had burned down in the late-eighteen-hundreds. Among the parishioners were the family Underwood. Father: Josiah; Mother: Joan; and six children: Ada, Billie (another girl), Albert, Cornelius, Persephone, and Frank.

It had to be a coincidence. Dig deep enough into history, and you're bound to find someone with the same name as yours. Dig even deeper, and you're likely to find your twin, as evidenced by that Facebook post I'd seen earlier with photographic evidence attesting to the fact Nicholas Cage was a time traveller.

For some reason, Seph and I seemed to live our lives outside of the digital limelight. There were no Facebook pages for Persephone/Seph Underwood and none for Addison/Addie Haney until a few days ago. My overall digital footprint was even smaller than Seph's, and the only Addie Haney with a web page wasn't me.

I stumbled upon Ancestry.ca and looked us up there, too, but there were no Persephone Underwoods listed, and the only Addison Haneys there were men.

Having come to the conclusion the Internet—that font of all knowledge—was a bust, I decided to contact Ontario's Ministry of Community and Social Services. Seph had told me, point blank, she'd worked there, so I was sure they'd be able to shed some light on her competency.

After sitting on hold for what seemed like a millennium, someone answered the phone, saying, "Community and Social Services. This is Jen. How may I help you?"

"Hello. I was wondering if I might be able to speak with Persephone Underwood."

"I'm sorry...who?"

Calm down, Addison. She probably misheard you.

I cleared my throat and repeated, "Persephone Underwood. She's my social worker."

"The name doesn't sound familiar, off-hand," the woman said. "Let me consult our records. Please hold."

Tinny Beatles music played *Eleanor Rigby* through the receiver.

"Hello, ma'am?" She cleared her throat. "I'm sorry, but we don't have a Persephone Underwood registered in our service."

"Could you check again? She goes by the name of Seph more often than not."

"Spell that for me?"

I did.

"Hold again?" She'd said it like a question, but before I could answer, she was gone. The music continued to play, but I didn't recognize the tune.

When she came back, she said, "I'm sorry, but no Seph Underwood either. No Underwoods of any name, I'm afraid."

I thanked her and hung up the phone.

If Seph was my friend, why hadn't she told me? If she were something more intimate, why hadn't she told me that either?

I'd spent the better part of the morning looking for answers and had come up less than empty with more questions than ever as to whom I was and how Seph and Piers figured into it.

My batting average sucked so far.

Strike one: though I'd discovered I was caffeine free, hated bananas, and I might be bi-curious if not bi-sexual, I still had no real idea who I was, nor did I know why I thought of my quest as a baseball game.

Strike two: I had no idea who Piers was to me, though I did know I wanted more of whatever I'd experienced the night before.

Strike three: I had no idea who Seph really was, nor did I have a handle on what she'd meant to me.

I refused to strike out while I was still at the plate.

Stoker's had been jumping after hours, and I hoped to get a look at it in the daylight, maybe go inside if it was open, and check it out with fresh eyes. Though the welts and blisters from my last foray into daylight had healed, I still worried about another painful reaction to the sun, so I put on a long-sleeved t-shirt with a picture of a white skull made from a series of flowers. I paired them with some ripped blue jeans and a pair of black, Tom's slip-ons, and checked myself out in the mirror. I looked as exhausted as I felt—no wonder, seeing as I'd only gotten two, maybe three hours' sleep at best before Seph had threatened to break my door down. All I needed to complete my outfit was a hat. I pulled one down from the top closet shelf, heard a huge smash, and turned to see that a shoebox had fallen to the floor, its contents spilled out around it. There wasn't much inside: a bunch of old and faded photographs, a safety deposit box key, a business card, and some old coins. I scooped the artifact collection back into the box, took it into my bedroom, and sat on the bed to take a closer look.

The pictures were from a number of decades. There were the sepia tones of the early nineteen-hundreds, the black and whites of the mid-nineteen-hundreds, faded Polaroids from the seventies, and snapshots from the eighties, with nothing more modern. The organization and proper analysis of the twenty or so photos would take more time than I had at that moment.

Like the pictures, the coins were from a number of decades, a few from the eighteen-hundreds, most from the early nineteen-hundreds.

The safety deposit key was interesting. Though I had no idea which bank it was from, I hoped it might, like the cheques, be from the CIBC down the street. Like the pictures, the sleuthing of the story behind the key would, unfortunately, have to happen at another time.

The business card, however—well, that was a horse of a different colour. The card was black—no surprise there. The name of the business, Pumpkin Spice & Everything Nice, was written on the card in large, orange letters transposed over a hugely grinning silver Jack-o-lantern. On the back was the slogan, "Coffee and the occult", an address, and a phone number. I decided I'd take a rain cheque on daytime Stoker's in favour of checking out the establishment on the card.

Pumpkin Spice & Everything Nice appeared to be a coffee shop from the outside. The signage above the door and window had the same lettering, logo, and slogan as on the card. Once I'd stepped inside, all questions as to how an independent coffee shop could possibly hope to survive amidst the Timothy's, Starbucks, Tim Hortons, and Second Cups in the downtown core disappeared.

True to their slogan, the shop was all coffee in the front, occult in the back. The back third of the store had an entirely different ambiance. Rather than a bank of coffee bean dispensers behind the service desk, there was a bank of mason jars on shelving. I imagined they contained things like eye of newt, toe of frog, and tongue of bat. At least one of them contained what looked like pig fetuses. I shuddered at the recognition, wondering if they actually brewed potions with them or if they were just for show. Besides myself, the establishment was devoid of customers—cue my earlier question about the viability of independent coffee shops.

On my way to the back of the shop, I passed a rack of t-shirts exactly the same as the one I was wearing. Though it could have been a co-incidence—the shirts were mass-produced and assumedly distributed to a number of similar stores across a wide area—a fleeting wave of déjà vu made its way through the back of my mind. I'd taken my hat off and put it on the counter in front of me when a woman came from behind me. She was in her twenties with hair—and maybe skin—bleached white and wearing too much black makeup around her lips and eyes. She also had a number of piercings—I counted at least ten in and around her ears and another five on her face. Her crowning glory was her earplugs, made of clear acrylic, and which seemed half-filled with blood. I imagined I could easily slip a quarter through those holes once the plugs had been removed and with room to spare.

Her face dropped when she went around to the proprietor's side of the counter and saw my face. "You're not supposed to be here," she said. Her eyes darted from side to side as if to make sure I was alone or that I hadn't been followed.

"You know me?" I asked.

"Let me guess: you're suffering buyer's remorse. I thought I made it clear the last time you were here: no backsies."

She turned to walk away, but I grabbed her arm from across the counter. "I was in here before?"

"You're suffering memory loss. I also made the side effects of the procedure clear: memory loss, photosensitivity, low iron, and unusual cravings. Like I told you before: they'll eventually pass."

"You performed a procedure on me? Here?"

She looked down at my hand on her arm and then looked back up at me. The skin where I'd pressed with my thumb had turned even whiter than the rest of her skin, which I wouldn't have thought possible, given her overall complexion.

I let go and took a quick look around. "What did you do to me? Did you curse me? Who ordered it?"

"Chillax, bitch," she said. "*I'm* not the one who cursed you."

"So what *did* you do?"

"Look, whatever I did came with a non-disclosure clause. I delivered services, you paid for services as rendered, end of story."

She turned to leave once more, and I grabbed her again, only this time, she spun around to face me. "I've just pressed the silent alarm, in case you're wondering, and now I have a gun pointed at your midsection behind the counter."

What she'd said scared me near senseless, but I wasn't about to back down. This woman knew what had happened to me; hell, she'd performed the procedure to put me in this state. I'd be damned if I'd leave before I had my answers.

"The police have quite a good response time in this neck of the woods," the salesperson told me. "The way I see it, this can go down two ways: either the police arrive and arrest your sorry ass for trespassing, harassment, and assault, or they arrive to find your rotting corpse on the floor. You decide."

When I let go of her arm, she took a step back and laid the gun on top of the counter. "Go. And don't ever come back."

I let out a snigger of exasperation, rolled my eyes, and shook my head. "I don't believe it," I said. "I'm drowning here because of something you did to me. All I want are some answers."

"You want some answers, why don't you ask your girlfriend? She's the one that brought you in here, after all."

"My girlfriend?"

She went on to describe Seph to a T. "Seriously, bitch," she continued, "you should go. The police will be here any minute," she paused to take a look at her bicep, where my thumb had left a nice mark, "and I have the bruises to prove assault."

"There's nothing more you can tell me?" I asked.

She shook her head. "You're in breach of contract, and I have a reputation to protect."

I gave the salesperson a look, left the shop, and headed for my car. When it was close enough to see, I halted dead in my tracks, unable to stop what had happened in the store from replaying in my mind. My eyes closed, I looked up to the sky, felt the burn of the sun, and realized I'd left my hat on the counter at the store. Betting on the fact the girl had been bluffing about the silent alarm, I headed back.

Pumpkin Spice & Everything Nice was as deserted as when I was there the first time—or had that been the second time?

"Hello?" I said, alerting the salesperson to my presence, but there was no answer.

"I don't want any trouble," I said, lest she follow through with her earlier threat to turn me into a rotting corpse. "I'll just take my hat and go." I walked to the occult section at the back of the store and screamed when I saw the salesperson lying on the floor in a pool of blood. Most of it seemed to have come from a gaping wound in her throat, which appeared to have been torn open. My belly churned, but I managed to swallow the bile collecting at the back of my throat.

My hat was still intact on the counter, though it had taken minor blood spatter. Police sirens sounded in the distance. I didn't have much time if I didn't want to be taken in and questioned for the girl's murder, so I grabbed my hat and went to duck out the back entrance, but my foot landed on a white, plastic hangar on the floor. I slipped, and my leg nearly gave out beneath me, but I caught my balance and avoided falling into the growing puddle of blood.

I was halfway to my car when I turned back again, curious to see how the situation had progressed. When I got there, a crowd had begun to gather outside of Pumpkin Spice & Everything Nice. A policeman was in the process of tying yellow police tape from one corner of the building to a sapling on the boulevard, across to a bicycle stand, and back to the adjacent corner of the building. Uniformed police officers stood sentry just inside the boundary, keeping onlookers at bay. A few black and white police vehicles had pulled in to barricade Yonge Street. Officers were standing outside their vehicles, putting on reflective vests and attempting to divert traffic down side streets.

"What happened?" I asked a voyeur, who shrugged his shoulders.

I made my way through the crowd with the intent of getting a better look.

A policewoman was questioning a woman just inside the yellow tape. "I heard a gunshot," the woman told the cop, "and then a scream. A few minutes later, I heard another scream."

"Did you see anything?" the policewoman asked.

The woman shook her head. "I called 911 after the first scream, but I was told a car had already been sent in response to a silent alarm."

The policewoman nodded and said, "Thank you for your help." She handed the witness a card. "If you think of anything else or want to learn of the progress of the case, you can call this number." The witness nodded, and the officer held the police tape up for her to crouch under.

I waited until I saw the salesgirl's body being taken out on a stretcher in a body bag.

She'd said Seph was the key.

It reminded me that I had an actual key. I needed to find that safety deposit box to see what was inside. It could wait; daylight wouldn't. My next stop had to be Stoker's in the daytime.

Stoker's looked like a dump in the daylight. The exterior was done up in stucco over the brick, painted black, and in desperate need of a touch-up. Bits and pieces of stucco had begun to spald, revealing tired, red brick that had also started to spald. A small, red laminated sign said they were open for business in large, white, block letters, so I went in.

The interior was much brighter than I'd remembered. Though it wasn't as busy as it had been the last time I was there, quite a few people were patronizing the joint, most of them dressed in business suits.

I wondered what they had on the menu and saddled up to the bar, surprised to see the same bartender on duty as the night before. He smiled at me in recognition.

"Back for more?" he said.

"Yeah, well…you know me—can't get enough of this place."

His smile seemed self-deprecating. "What can I get you?"

"Can you do a virgin of the drink I had last night? No alcohol."

"A non-alcoholic, virgin martini?"

"I'll just have a Coke."

"Coming right up."

I checked the place out. Gone were the DJ, the cliques of people dressed in various shades of black, and the people writhing on the floor in ecstasy, whether real or substance-induced. Eighties Muzak played soft and low through hidden speakers.

"One Coke," the bartender said, drawing my attention. "Piers isn't here."

"I kind of figured." I took a sip of my drink.

"While we're on the subject," I continued, "what can you tell me about Piers?"

"Aww, you know Piers." He pulled a dishtowel from under the counter and wiped the bar down.

"Actually, I don't." I looked into my glass, stirring the ice with the straw. "I had some sort of accident. I don't remember."

"What happened?" He stopped rubbing the towel on the bar and gave me his full attention.

I just looked at him.

"Right," he said after a moment. "Because you don't remember."

I nodded. "I'm on a quest for clues that'll jog my memory. Anything you can tell me—"

"I can't," he said. "I signed a non-disclosure agreement." Another NDA—what was it about my life and the people in it that was so secretive?

The bartender resumed rubbing the counter. "What happens in Stoker's stays in Stoker's."

I gave a laugh and looked to my left and right. "We *are* in Stoker's."

"I can't," he apologized. "Breaking my NDA's punishable by slow and painful death that would reverberate down through the generations of my family, if and when I have one." He'd said that last part way too seriously.

"You do that a lot, you know," I said, stirring the pot, "say people will kill you if you do something they wouldn't like."

"Only because it's true. People *literally* get killed for crossing Stoker's establishment and patrons."

Piers was a patron of the bar. According to what I'd learned after talking to him, *I'd* crossed him, and I was still standing. I decided not to correct the bartender.

"Does your NDA include talking to patrons about themselves?"

"I don't know…"

"What can you tell me about *me*?"

"I don't know if I can."

"I promise not to tell."

"It's not you I'm afraid of." His eyes darted back and forth as if checking to make sure no one else was within hearing distance. "The walls have eyes," he whispered.

Though I found his response comically cliché, I managed to stifle the guffaw building behind my lips. "Ears."

"Huh?"

"The saying is the walls have ears."

He stopped wiping the counter and looked at me through squinted eyes. "No, that doesn't sound right," he said after a beat, and he went back to cleaning the bar.

"*Please*," I begged.

The bartender sighed in resignation. "You're in here with Piers practically every night."

"Tell me something I don't know," I said, sounding defeated. Why didn't anyone want to talk to me? Why would no one help me?

"Let's just say, if you've lost your memory, consider yourself lucky where Piers and his merry band of followers are concerned. Leave Stoker's and your boyfriend behind."

"Piers is my *boyfriend*?" I asked. "How do you know?" As if our behaviour on the dance floor hadn't been evidence enough.

"I have to go," he said. "I've said too much already." He and his towel were at the other side of the bar in a flash.

I took another sip of my drink, my eyes following the bottles in the well-stocked bar to the television mounted in the corner. The news was on. A reporter was standing in front of a store, the unmistakable orange Comic Sans lettering of Pumpkin Spice & Everything Nice in the background. "Hey," I called to the bartender, "turn that up."

"...and police found the body in response to a silent alarm that had been sounded.

"Yonge Street is closed in both directions for the ongoing investigation," the reporter said. "Though there were working surveillance cameras on site, none of them were in the back room where the employee was killed, and there is no footage from the cameras in the front of the store, due to an EMF interruption that seemed to affect all cameras in the area, including CCTV cameras on the street, the result of suspected solar flare activity.

"Witnesses report hearing a gunshot and two screams, moments apart. Police are waiting for the autopsy to determine if this is, indeed, the thirty-sixth homicide of the year. They're asking anyone who was in the area to come forward with what they saw by calling Crime Stoppers at 416-222-TIPS.

"On Yonge Street, I'm Aadhya Sidana, Citypulse News."

The news report continued, but I signalled to the bartender that I'd heard enough.

I'd been in the area. Hell, I'd been right in the store moments before and after it had happened, and I saw nothing. My instinct to duck out the back door had served me well. It was also serendipitous there had been solar flares at that precise moment. It meant no one could place me anywhere near the store. It also meant I wouldn't be questioned as a witness.

I shuddered at the thought I'd come this close to being the victim of a double-homicide. My body gave another involuntary shudder at the realization that the silent alarm had been real, and I'd come just as close to being arrested and questioned as the prime suspect in the salesperson's murder.

Had the perpetrator been lying in wait in the store while I was there? If so, it meant the murderer might recognize me. If the murderer could identify me, he might come after me in an attempt to eliminate all witnesses.

It also meant I might be in danger for real.

I signalled the bartender again. "How much do I owe you?" I asked.

"I put it on Piers' tab," he said.

I left my tip on the bar, made a mental note to thank Piers the next time I saw him, and I left for home.

I kind of hoped Piers would call me. We'd gotten pretty close on the dance floor the night before. The day had been kind of a bust, and the call would've been a welcome diversion, for no reason than to have a chance to pump him for information. I wished I'd had the foresight to ask him for his number—I wasn't above calling him myself.

Seph had already called me a number of times, and I'd sent them all to voicemail, unsure if I'd ever retrieve them. Having established she wasn't really my social worker—or a social worker at all, for that matter—she was, at best, a clingy friend and at worst, a possessive (maybe ex-) lover. I planned to avoid her as best I could until I had more of my situation figured out.

Whether or not Piers would call, it was getting late—it was already 8:00 p.m., and I'd had less than three hours' sleep over the past forty-eight hours. I found a pair of sweats in the bureau drawer, changed into them, brushed my teeth, washed my face, and put my hair up in a high ponytail. There hadn't been enough time to remedy the television problem in my bedroom, so I went to a local channel's website on my phone and browsed recent shows, hoping to stream one of them as a diversion, when there was a knock at my door. I decided to ignore it at first, but then whoever it was knocked again, a bit more forcefully. Seph had caused so much of a commotion when she'd done the same earlier in the day, so I went to see who it was, for no other reason than to save my neighbours a call to management.

There was a strange man through the peephole when I checked. It wasn't saying much—pretty much every man I saw was a stranger these days.

I threw open all of the bolt-locks on the door but kept the chain on, opened the door, and peeked through the crack. "Can I help you?" I asked.

"Addison Haney?" he said.

"Who wants to know?

"Piers sent me."

"For what?"

"Please, open the door."

Anyone could have said he'd been sent by Piers. I'd already had one close call that day, back at the Pumpkin Spice, and I wasn't about to chance another. "I'm going to need proof you are who you say you are."

The man sighed, shifted something he was carrying—though I couldn't tell what from my vantage point—and took a cell phone out from his jacket pocket. He speed-dialed someone, said, "She needs proof, sir," once the call had connected, and handed the phone to me.

"Addie?" Piers said through the line. He continued, sort of breathy, "God, it sounds so strange to call you that." In his normal tone, he continued, "Let the man in, sweetie. I sent him to bring you to me."

"What do you *usually* call me?" I asked.

"We can speak of that later."

"We can speak of it now, or I'm not going with him." One way or another, I *would* get my answers.

"Addison Haney," he started, as if he were my father about to scold me, "you will let my servant in, get dressed, and let him escort you to me. We will speak of other things at another time. Are we clear?"

The only things clear were that Piers was being evasive, and I was exhausted. I opened my mouth to tell him where to go but said, "Clear," instead. Before I knew it, the chain was off the door. The man stood there as if awaiting permission to enter.

"Piers?" I said into the phone, but he'd disconnected.

"Well," I said to the man, "are you coming in or not?"

He took a step into the apartment, swung a garment bag from over his shoulder, held it out to me, and said, "Piers requests you wear this attire. He also requests matching heels and full makeup."

"Oh, he does, does he?" I stared him down. He stared back at me, without blinking once. When it was clear I wasn't about to win the game, I acquiesced.

"Wait here," I said, trying not to sound defeated. I shut the door behind the guy, leaving it purposely unlocked in case I had to make a quick getaway, and went down the hall to get dressed.

A half-hour and three pairs of ripped stockings later, and I was ready to go. Piers had sent a blood red, three-quarter length, form-fitting dress. It had spaghetti straps and a bustier so tight, I wouldn't have to worry about a bra to hold me in place. I found a pair of medium-high, black, strappy pumps, a black, three-quarter sleeve, knit bolero shrug, and beaded, black clutch in the closet, and went to meet Piers' "servant".

It was a strange way to refer to someone in your employ, "servant", connoting that he had no choice but to serve. I thought about how Piers had convinced me to let his man in and to go with him, using no more than the tone of his voice, and I couldn't help but wonder if I'd been his servant, too. A servant with benefits. The thought was enough to make me cringe, no matter how titillated I'd felt in his presence.

The car Piers had sent for me was, surprisingly, a white Lincoln Town Car with a white leather interior and seats, and a fully stocked bar in the back. There was a window tinted dark separating the front seat from the back which seated six, three facing the front of the car, three facing the back.

Piers' man lowered the window halfway and said, "Shall I turn on the music?"

"No," I told him, "I'm good."

"Very well," he said. "Help yourself to the bar," and he put the window up again.

We set out driving north, but rather than continue up Yonge Street to Stoker's—where I'd assumed we were headed—he got on the Gardiner Expressway and headed west. Feeling a little worried, I knocked on the window. The driver lowered it to half-mast again. "We're not going to Stoker's," I told him.

"No, ma'am. Stoker's is closed for the evening."

"Why?"

"Police investigation." He began to raise the window.

"What?" I asked. The window had clicked into place, so I knocked on it again. He lowered it, and I said, "What happened?"

"The bartender was murdered." He paused before saying, "Horribly."

"Oh, my God." I felt sick in the pit of my stomach. I'd been there only a few hours before. For all I knew, the murderer had been right there in the bar with me.

Right there in the bar—hadn't I made the same supposition earlier in the day at the Pumpkin Spice? Was someone following me? Had they killed the salesgirl and bartender to keep them from telling my secrets?

I leaned back in my seat. More than likely, it had been a coincidence. I was a nobody who knew nothing. Why would anyone want to follow me—scared, confused, amnesiac me—let alone kill innocents I'd interacted with?

Piers didn't strike me as a nobody. In fact, he struck me as quite the somebody, with minions to populate his entourage, servants to do his bidding at his beckon call, and me, jumping at the drop of a hat when summoned for a booty call. Maybe the killings had something to do with my association with Piers.

He'd promised me answers on the phone earlier. I could only hope he was about to make good on the promise.

We pulled up in front of a five-star hotel in Toronto's west end near Pearson Airport. The driver lowered the window once more and handed me an envelope containing a key card. "Piers is waiting for you in the room on the envelope," he said. He raised the window before I could thank him. The doorman opened the car door, gave me his hand to help me out, got back into the car, and pulled away the second the door had closed behind him.

The interior of the hotel was shiny surface overkill. Whatever surface hadn't been gold-plated was covered in mirrors or marble. People milled about in the lobby wearing mostly business attire. There wasn't a single child in sight. Uniformed employees stood at attention at their posts, ready to spring into action at the first indication of a patron in need of assistance.

Piers' hotel room was on the top floor of the building. The elevator doors were stainless steel, polished to mirror perfection. When the doors parted, I was surprised to see a uniformed employee operating the elevator. "Penthouse," I told him.

"As you wish," he said with a nod and was silent until the doors opened again. "Penthouse," he informed me and fell silent once more.

I thanked him, went to Piers' room, and knocked on the door.

When he opened it, the first thing I felt was panic—I found myself staring at one of the most beautiful creatures I'd ever seen. To call him pretty would not have been an understatement; he was dressed to the nines in a tuxedo, complete with bowtie, unravelled, and hung around his neck.

"There you are. Didn't my driver give you the keycard?"

I held it up to show him. "I wouldn't feel comfortable just walking in."

He flashed me a grin and retreated, turning when he reached the rough centre of the room. "Do I have to invite you in?"

"No, I just…"

"No need to stand on ceremony, then." He came back to me, took my hand, and pulled me into the room, shutting the door behind us.

Had I thought the place to be a room? Once inside, I saw it was a four-room, two-bedroom, two-bathroom plus kitchenette suite. There was a small dining table near the window on the far side of the room with several cloched plates. I suddenly felt as uncomfortable as Julia Roberts when she met up with Richard Gere to render services. It didn't help I was wearing a dress as red and form-fitting as hers had been in the movie.

"You look nothing short of breathtaking," he told me.

"Yeah, I threw on the first dress I could find," I said, hoping to alleviate the tension.

"I thought we'd stay in tonight. Get to know each other again." He walked over to the table.

"Aren't we a little overdressed to be saying in?"

"This," he waved a hand to indicate the hotel room, "is whatever we make it." He removed the cloche from one of the plates to reveal chocolate covered strawberries, arranged in a series of concentric circles. The centre ring looked to be covered in dark chocolate with sea salt, the middle ring was covered in white chocolate, and the outer in milk chocolate. Piers handed me a champagne flute, picked up a white chocolate-covered strawberry, brought it to my lips, and I took a bite. The strawberry was firm and sweet. It had made its own liqueur when covered with the chocolate. Some of it dripped down my chin and Piers reached out and caught it with his thumb. He brought his thumb to his mouth and sucked it clean.

I didn't know whether to be aroused or grossed out by the gesture and smiled at him uncomfortably. When I sipped the champagne, it was incredibly sweet, enhanced by the lingering berry juice on my tongue.

Piers uncovered another plate—raw oysters on the half-shell.

Aphrodisiacs. He was feeding me Aphrodisiacs.

I *was* Pretty Woman to his Richard Gere, and I didn't like it one bit.

"I'm not eating that," I told him.

"Why not?"

"Why did you ask me here tonight, Piers?"

"I told you: to get to know each other again."

"Know each other as in the biblical sense?"

He brought a hand to his heart and affected a wounded look. "I am hurt that you would question my motives."

I felt bad for not trusting him. Then again, why *should* I trust him? Outside of a wonderfully erotic make-out session on the dance floor the night before, I really didn't know much about the man. "You're right," I said. "I'm sorry for questioning you, but I'm still not putting that into my mouth."

He downed the oyster, chuckled, and said, "Fair enough."

The final cloche covered a plate of halved fresh figs, drizzled in honey, sprinkled with feta cheese, and topped with pomegranate arils. "Figs?" I asked. "What's all this about, Piers?"

"More questions, my dear?"

"You said you wanted to get to know me. Let's talk and get to know each other."

"Very well," he said, sitting. "But please, try the figs. I had the chef prepare them special."

"Fine." I lifted one from the plate and took a bite. A drop of honey dribbled onto my chin.

Rather than reach over again, Piers said, "You have something…" and he indicated by pointing to his own chin. I reached up and tried to wipe it off, but he said, "No, the other side." Once more, I tried to wipe it off, evidently missing it entirely because he said, "Here, let me."

He stood up and leaned forward as if to use his thumb but swooped in at the last second and used his lips and tongue to lap the honey clean.

My first reaction was to jump up and away from his snake-like move, but then his lips moved to mine. His tongue brushed mine, and I tasted honey.

When our lips parted, I could do nothing but look into his deep emerald eyes and sigh.

"Shall we move to the bedroom?" he asked.

I hadn't planned for there to be any physical contact that night. As far as I was concerned, it was nothing more than a recon mission, designed to collect intelligence on Piers—who he was, both in life and to me. Instead, I'd found myself in the midst of a re-enactment of the night before. His kiss had been intoxicating. No matter how much I tried to resist, like a junkie, I needed another fix.

He took my hand, led me to the bedroom, and lay me down on the king-sized bed. I felt my dress fall from my shoulders and wondered when he'd undone the zipper in the back—he was nothing if not fast, I'd give him that.

I remembered I hadn't worn a bra and my hand went up to cover my breasts.

"Uh, uh, uh," Piers said, his eyes meeting mine. "No self-consciousness allowed."

I nodded in spite of myself and reached for his jacket lapels. He helped me slide the jacket off.

"You are so beautiful." He trailed kisses across my shoulders, his lips coming to rest on my neck.

I undid the buttons of his shirt as he kissed my neck. When I tugged at the shirt, he took it off and pressed his hard chest against mine, while sucking on the lobe of my ear.

He pushed himself up into a full-plank position and looked me in the eyes. "You have to give consent. I will not take anything from you that you do not want to give," he said.

Was that his way of asking if I wanted to have sex?

He dropped his knee between my legs and pressed.

Did I *want* to have sex?

He pulled his knee away and pressed it back as he trailed his tongue from the base of my ear to the crook of my neck; the experience was nothing short of ecstasy. Just as suddenly as he'd escalated my libido, he stopped, did a sort of push-up to prop himself up again, and waited for my answer.

There was only one thing I could say.

"You have my consent." Okay, so maybe romance wasn't my bag, but I could think of nothing else to say, as my brain had ceased all rational thought and was no longer in control of my body.

Piers' driver dropped me at my condo just after sunrise the next morning. When I entered my unit, I was surprised to see Seph inside, lying on the chaise lounge in the room. Though I was livid, I decided not to fight her about it. "Knock much?" I asked.

"What, and miss your walk of shame?"

She was right. It was all I could think about on the drive home. I barely knew Piers and yet the things we did? Oh, what we did!

"What's that on your neck?" she asked, sitting up.

My hand found a scratch on the left side of my neck. "Piers went to put my hair behind my ear, and he scratched me. He felt awful about it. It was so cute; he even offered to kiss it better—"

"And did he? Kiss it better?"

I didn't see it as any of her business, but I answered anyway. "Well, yes. As a matter of fact, he did."

"Stupid," Seph muttered under her breath.

Though I'd heard her perfectly, I said, "What did you say?"

She stood and took a few steps closer to me. "It was stupid to let him taste your blood."

"He didn't *taste* my blood," I told her. That would have been gross.

"If you say so."

Up until then, I was standing in the entryway, but I took a few steps into the apartment, crossed my arms over my chest, and said, "You're upset."

"I was worried."

"Who, exactly, are we to each other?" I asked.

"I'm your—"

"Social worker—so you've said. Trouble is, Social Services has no record of you working there." I started to pace. "Cut the crap, Seph—we were together once, weren't we?"

She looked at me as if weighing whether to tell me the truth and if so, exactly how much. "A lifetime ago, yes."

I stopped pacing and turned to face her. "Did I leave you for Piers?"

She shook her head. "We were over long before you met Piers."

"Piers and I were together…before?"

"Yes."

"I don't understand. Why are you so opposed to my being with him?"

Seph walked directly to me, took my face in her hands, and said, "Things are different. You're more…fragile now."

"Piers doesn't want to hurt me," I said.

She embraced me and whispered, "Things could get dangerous for you if you insist on hanging with him." She went back to the chaise to get her purse. On her way out, she stopped to kiss me on the cheek. "I'm just glad you're okay." She left before I could ask her any more questions.

After sleeping most of the day away, I fried up a few eggs and toasted some bread. Though I felt stronger after eating, I was antsy in the apartment. There were only so many *Supernatural* episodes you could binge before you questioned why, if there were so many monsters out there, the world remained in darkness where their existence was concerned.

Night had begun to fall. I wanted to go somewhere I could let it all hang out and be myself, whoever that might be. If I happened to run into Piers along the way, then so be it.

Stoker's looked as it should in the darkness: nondescript and under the radar of the general populace. Upon closer examination, it seemed run-down and dead. Once inside, however, it was a different story. Though it was too early to be at full capacity, quite a few people were already sitting at the bar, at the tables, or on the dance floor.

I pushed through the people at the bar to order a drink, but before I could, the bartender—a woman, this time—said, "Bloodberry martini coming up." The drink was on the counter in front of me before I could blink. "Piers isn't here yet," she told me. The last bartender had greeted me with an update of Piers' whereabouts, too.

"I heard about your colleague," I told her.

"Bummer, huh?"

"I'm sorry for your loss."

"Huh? Oh, thanks." Someone summoned her from the other side of the bar. "You okay for now?"

I told her that I was, and she went to the other customer.

It hadn't been that long since I'd spoken to the bartender that had been killed. When I'd met him, he'd said, "Piers would literally kill me if I didn't treat you right."

He'd also said I should leave Stoker's, Piers, and his entourage behind, and that the walls had ears.

At the time, I hadn't taken any of what he'd said seriously, but what if Piers had somehow heard what he'd said to me and lashed out?

Seph had told me Piers was dangerous, especially for me.

Could Piers have been responsible for the bartender's death?

I chugged the martini and signaled for another; I chugged that one, too.

The DJ played Siouxsie and the Banshees' cover of *Dear Prudence*. It was an odd song for a nightclub, but maybe psychedelic seventies music was a part of the whole Goth bar scene—who was I to judge? Before the first chorus, I was up on the dance floor, moving to the beat. When Siouxsie repeated the words, "look around," I closed my eyes, felt my arms raise to the sky as if levitating, and heard a scream.

I opened my eyes to pandemonium. Everyone ran for cover while I remained frozen in place in the rough centre of the dance floor. A few people were on the floor, most probably knocked down in the stampede during the mass exodus from the building. Whether they were still alive was anyone's guess.

A brush of cool air went past me, and I looked up to see a wisp of smoke materialize near the disco ball suspended from the ceiling. The smoke cloud expanded until it hung in the air like a fog, and then it took off, drawing a large circle around the dance floor and meandering about the remaining patrons. It circled the dance floor once more, seemed to solidify into a vapour trail, and came right at me.

In the split second before the vapour hit me, I swear I saw my face reflected in it, like a projection on a screen in too much light, and then I experienced crystal clarity.

For the first time since I'd woken up with amnesia, I knew who I was, who Piers was, who Seph was—hell, I knew who Piers' sycophant, Percival, was. I also remembered each and every encounter I'd had with the proprietor of the Pumpkin Spice, including the miasma that had sent me to her in the first place.

And just like that, it was gone. Before I knew it, I was on the ground with the air knocked from me.

The fact that someone was on top of me didn't help my breathing situation any.

When I opened my eyes, Piers' face was hovering above mine. "Miss me?" he asked with a smile.

Black spots threatened to overtake my vision, and I felt lightheaded. "Can't…breathe," I managed.

"Sorry." He climbed off of me.

I looked up in time to see the cloud of smoke dissipate. Piers helped me to stand, and I checked out the dance floor. The people that had been knocked to the floor were gone. So were half of the patrons.

"What was that?" I asked Piers. "What just happened?"

He signalled a server who was shuddering in fear against the bar. "You look like you could use a drink." He took me by the elbow and led me to a booth in the corner.

I sat on the edge of the seat, trying to make myself small, my body shaking uncontrollably. Piers put a hand on my shoulder, reminding me he was there. I turned toward him and said, "What *was* that?

Piers made shushing noises.

"Seriously...what *was* that?" I shuddered and fought to catch my breath.

Piers took my chin in his hand, stared at me with those greener than green eyes, and said, "Calm down, Addison." I thought I saw him wince at the sound of my name. "You must breathe."

"I...I...I can't," I managed through sobs. How could I breathe when my body was racked by a fear so deep, it was petrified?

"You must take a deep breath."

I shook my head and pulled from his grasp.

"Addison," he said my name so low I almost didn't hear him. "Addison," he said loudly, forcefully, and I turned. Once more, he took my chin in his hand, looked me in the eye, and said, "You must breathe. Long and slow. Breathe in."

Though my breath hitched halfway through, I felt my lungs fill with air as if compelled to do so.

"Breathe out," Piers commanded, and I did.

Before I knew it, my breathing had returned to normal, and I felt much calmer.

"Better?"

I nodded my head. "Better," I confirmed.

He leaned against the deep, plush, velveteen chair, put an arm on my shoulder, and pulled me back into his embrace. I sat there a moment, my head against Piers' chest as he stroked my hair. "Now," he said, "about what you saw—"

"It was like vapour, but cold, like an icy wind." I wanted to sit up to look at him, but he held my body fast against his. "It seemed…sentient, somehow…human. It hit me—no—it travelled *through* me, and I sensed its thoughts.

"I know how crazy that sounds, but—"

"It does not sound crazy," he said.

"You believe me?"

"I believe that is what you think you saw—"

"Don't patronize me, Piers," I said, sliding forward on the seat.

He strengthened his hold on my shoulder and pulled me back. "I am not," he said. "I believe you have had a lot to drink. You were on a crowded dance floor with strobing lights. I believe you did see something like a vapour, but it was nothing more than the fog machine. You might have thought you saw a face in it, but that is what they call pareidolia—when your brain sees things and tries to find patterns in it, like those people who think they see Jesus on a slice of toast."

I shook my head. "It spoke to me, Piers," I told him. What, exactly, it had said teased the back of my speech centre, daring it to remember.

Piers smiled at me. "What did it say?"

"Now you're taunting me."

He let out a breath of air. "Not at all." I tried to break free from his grip again, and he pulled me back once more. "I am not," he said with empathy.

A waiter brought over a tray of shot glasses. Piers gave a nod as if to thank him, picked up one of the glasses, and handed it to me. "Drink this."

I looked into his eyes. "You already said I've had too much to drink."

"This will help; hair of the dog." He returned my gaze and said, "Drink up."

I took the glass from him and did as he'd said. When I was done, I put the glass back on the table and leaned into him, closing my eyes. The music started up again: *Spectre* by Radiohead.

That was it!

The word tickling the tip of my tongue. "What's a spectre?" I asked Piers. The additional alcohol had begun to work its way through my system, eating away at the fear I'd felt earlier.

"You mean besides the title of this song?"

"I'm serious," I told him. "Is it like a ghost?"

I felt him shake his head. "A ghost is a disembodied spirit who has yet to cross over; a spectre is a disembodied spirit in search of a receptacle."

"Of a what?" This time I did pull free from his grasp to sit up and look at him directly.

"Of a place to call home."

"Like a building to haunt?"

Piers smiled as if amused. His eyes lit up, changing colour from intense emerald to bright turquoise. "Like a body."

When the…spectre had smashed into me, I'd seen its face, that of a young woman with features similar to mine. While it was inside me, there was this odd sense of peace, of cognizance with my place in the world. Once it had left, I was an empty vessel, alone in the world without purpose.

"The spectre I saw…it's mine, isn't it?"

"Whoa, whoa, whoa," he said, leaning forward, forcing me to do the same. "Who said what you saw was anything remotely like a spectre?"

Another thought struck me. "How do you know about spectres anyway, Piers? What aren't you telling me?"

"I read. And there is nothing I am not telling you."

I closed my eyes and shook my head. Something was off about Piers, about our relationship, about…everything, since I'd met him.

"Hey," he said.

I turned away from him and continued to shake my head.

"Hey," he said more forcefully. This time I did turn. "It is not a spectre." I looked away again, contemplating how long I should wait before I got up and walked away.

"Look at me," he said, and I did. "It is not a spectre. Ghosts, spectres…they are things of dreams and nightmares. They are not real. What you saw was nothing more than the play of light on the fog. Okay?"

My first reaction was to insist what I saw was more than a trick of smoke, lights, and alcohol. I'd seen something in that cloud of fog, something that was alive; I knew it.

"Okay?" Piers repeated. He flashed me a glimpse of his gorgeous greens, and my previous thought process was lost.

"Okay," I replied.

"Okay," he confirmed.

I awoke the next morning to the sound of police sirens and looked out my window to see Piers' car in the centre of the commotion. I dressed frantically and went to see what had happened.

Maybe it wasn't Piers' car, I reasoned on my way down the elevator. The waterfront was prime real estate, even if it was stacked high above the ground. There had to be tons of people with town cars in the area.

There were a number of uniformed police officers in the lobby, talking to residents. I managed to slip by them to go outside.

Piers' driver was sitting in the front seat of his car. His head lolled back and to the side against the headrest. Blood seeped from a wound on his neck. It dripped onto his white shirt collar, turning it vivid crimson. When I was as close to the police tape cordoning off the scene as I could get, I peeked into the backseat and breathed a sigh of relief when I saw it was empty—no Piers.

Glad I'd had the prescience of mind to bring my phone with me, I tried to call Piers. Strange: I couldn't find his number in my contacts list. I remembered speaking to him on a cell phone and checked my call history, but then it dawned on me: I hadn't spoken to him on *my* cell phone. When he'd ordered up his booty call, it had been on his driver's phone, which meant my fingerprints would be all over it. The police were bound to find the phone and dust for prints, sooner or later.

The thought of the body count mounting around me was nauseating.

I wondered if it had been Piers. The girl at the Pumpkin Spice obviously had something to do with my current state of confusion, and my talk with the bartender could have been construed as flirtation—but why the driver? I'd had no contact with him other than the times Piers had sent him to get me.

The only other common thread was me. As little as I knew about Piers, I knew even less about myself. I didn't feel like a murderer. There was no bloodlust hidden inside of me, no thirst for blood, as far as I could tell.

Therein lay the problem: I couldn't tell. I'd half-convinced myself I was possessed by something like a spectre before Piers had stepped in to calm me down.

And while the fact I'd known all three victims could have been a coincidence, it became harder and harder to believe, given the rising body count.

The phrase, once is chance, twice is coincidence, three times is a pattern, popped into my head.

Once: the girl at the Pumpkin Spice. It could have been a chance occurrence. The downtown core of any city can be a dangerous place for a young girl, especially when she works at a coffee shop alone. Add to that the fact she'd dabbled in the occult and any number of things could have been responsible for her death.

Twice: the bartender at Stoker's. It could have been a coincidence. Stoker's patrons tended toward the Goth. They glorified death and embraced the emo side of life, which was sometimes mistaken for depression. But given the way he'd died, the bartender's death couldn't have been a suicide.

Three times: Piers' chauffeur outside my condo building. I didn't know anything about him—I didn't even know his name—but just like the other two deaths, I'd been the last person to see him alive, outside of the killer.

There were too many blanks in my life story to piece the puzzle together; I needed help.

I called Seph's phone, but there was no answer.

There were few numbers in my cell phone, but one of them was Dr. Putnum, the psychiatrist I'd spoken to at the hospital right after my "accident". Rather than call, hoping to score an appointment, I thought I might have a better chance of seeing her if I showed up on her doorstep.

I managed to find her office easily enough, but it was empty, so I sat on the floor, my back against the closed office door, browsing my Flipboard account until she came back. Over an hour later, my bum was looking at numb in the rearview mirror, and I was contemplating leaving when I heard, "Janet?"

I looked up to see Dr. Putnum, wearing a white lab coat and holding a stack of files in the crook of her elbow, which surprised me—didn't all doctors use tablets like on television these days?

I smiled at her and stood. "It's Addison, now. They found my identification."

"I like that," she said with a smile. "What can I do for you, dear?"

"Could I have a few minutes of your time to talk?"

She raised her eyebrows. "This is highly unusual, Ja—Addison."

"Please, Doctor."

"Without an appointment…and even then…"

"Coffee's on me?"

"I usually only cater to in-patients."

"I could check myself in for the day."

She paused as if weighing my offer. "I do have a break that's past due, now…Give me a minute."

There was a Starbucks in the hospital lobby. Oddly enough, Dr. Putnum ordered a pumpkin spice latte. In honour of my first "victim"—for that's how I thought of the three poor souls who had lost their lives for nothing more than being in my vicinity—I did the same.

We took a seat at a small, round table just outside of the coffee shop, such as it was. Dr. Putnum said, "So, Addison—do we have a last name?"

"Haney." I sipped my latte, wondering if I'd ever had real pumpkin pie and if I'd liked it.

"Where are you staying these days?"

"My condo. My keys and address were in my purse. I should mention they found my purse, too."

Dr. Putnum took sips of her latte between nods. "Any memories returned?"

I thought of the moment of clarity I'd experienced in Stoker's and the spectre I'd thought I'd seen and shook my head. "Nothing concrete. Mostly fleeting, ghostly images. I've reconnected with my best friend and boyfriend, though, so I'm not alone."

"Any family?"

"I don't think I have any."

Dr. Putnum looked down at the cup between her hands. "I'm sorry to hear that."

I shrugged.

"What did you want to talk about, Addison?"

I took a deep breath and let it out with a shrug. "Where do I begin?"

"Let's try at the beginning. Chronologically."

"At the beginning." I took a sip of my latte. "I found the card of this shop downtown, half-coffee shop, half-occult store—"

"Occult store?" she said, sounding surprised.

"I know. I frequent this Goth club, too, apparently—who knew?

"Anyway, I go to this store, and the salesgirl is scared of me. She's evasive, too. Claims she signed this non-disclosure agreement and can't tell even me what I was up to the last time I was there. I forgot my hat, and when I went back, the police were there, and she was dead—"

"Oh, dear—"

"It wasn't me," I said quickly. "At least...I don't *think* it was me. Her throat had been ripped out. I can't see how I could've done it without being covered in her blood."

"Wait...I heard that on the news. The store was the pumpkin something—"

"Pumpkin Spice & Everything Nice."

"Right." She took another sip of her coffee. "And it was really an occult store?"

"I was just as surprised as you."

"The murderer must've just missed you. I can see why you'd have the need to talk to someone."

"There's more."

"Oh?"

"I told you about the Goth bar I frequent—it's this place called Stoker's—"

"Oh, that's clever." I must've looked at her like I didn't understand why it was clever, because she said, "After Bram Stoker? *Dracula*?" When I didn't pick up my end of the conversation, she continued, "It's considered a trend-setting Gothic horror novel."

Something inside me clicked. It was like I'd known that bit of trivia but only remembered it after she'd said it. I smiled and said, "I get the reference.

"Anyway, the bartender at the club acts like he remembers me and serves me up this drink that I really liked. I went back the next day to talk to him, and he turns up dead later, in the same way as the Pumpkin Spice's barista."

"And you think *you* might've killed them?"

"I don't *think* I killed them, but if I didn't, then I'm either cursed or have pretty crappy luck; last night, my boyfriend's driver turned up dead in front of my building, still in his car—"

"Killed the same, messy way?"

"Yep." I leaned back in my seat and took a long sip of my drink.

"Sounds more like the people around you have crappy luck."

"That's a joke, right?"

"More like an observation."

"You know what, Doctor? I probably shouldn't have come here. People around me get killed. I've only put your life in danger by coming here. I should go before it's too late."

"Relax, Addison. I don't think there's a time limit on this, like seven minutes is okay, but eight is the kiss of death.

"Let's look at the facts: you have no recollection of committing these murders, and you're not covered in blood afterward. You don't have a pile of bloody clothing lying somewhere in your apartment, do you?"

"Not that I know of."

"And you're not experiencing blackouts, episodes of missed time?"

"No."

"The only missing memories are the ones *before* your mishap and not after?"

"That's right."

"Then I don't think it's you.

"Look," she said, cupping her drink between her hands and leaning forward over the table, "you came to me for help, not seeking absolution, which is what people who commit these types of crimes usually want. Either that or they want help to stop doing whatever it is they're doing. You've come here looking for neither."

That would have made sense if I knew who I was—I mean, who I truly was—before. I barely even knew myself now. I was worried about what had been happening around me, and if I was worried, it meant I had doubts.

She was right about one thing: I'd sought her out for answers, not forgiveness.

"What do you know about spectres?" I asked. It was a shot in the dark, but while I was there laying everything on the line, I thought I'd go for broke.

"As in ghosts?"

"Sort of. Crazy, I know—"

"Crazy's my business."

I must've looked confused, because she said, "Inside joke and in bad taste. Sorry."

"Is it normal to feel sort of...haunted in a situation like mine."

"Explain."

"I feel like there's something following me lately."

"Paranoia?"

"I don't think so. I don't think someone's *actually* following me. It's more like...I sense it."

She smiled in what I thought was an attempt to soothe rather than mock. "It's normal to feel like two people: the person you were before and the person you are now. It's possible what you sense is the person you were before. Maybe it's your memories knocking on the door—"

"I feel like the spectre's whispering to me, seeking possession."

Dr. Putnum took another sip of her latte, put it down, and gave me another of those smiles. "Your mind's speaking to you in metaphors. It's the sign of a creative person. It's normal for memories to want to return in cases like yours.

"Our brains are always re-wiring themselves in weird ways. You suffer from a sort of...memory aphasia. People with aphasia usually suffer language deficits, problems with speaking, listening, and writing. If they work hard at it, they can...re-train their brains to make new connections, sort of like workarounds for their problems. Maybe what you're experiencing is your brain in the process of building a bridge to your memories.

"Think of what you call your spectre akin to your memories tapping on the door of your brain—tickling your mind's eye, if you will. Eventually, the taps will grow to knocks and then even louder until you have no choice but to let them in."

"So, I'm not going crazy?"

She shook her head. "Take it from someone who knows." She winked.

"Do you remember the visualization exercises we did when you were in the hospital?"

I nodded.

"You might want to try that in an effort to speed up the process. Close your eyes. Imagine standing in front of a door. Try to imagine your memories on the other side. When you believe them to have fully manifested, open the door to invite them in."

I agreed I'd try, hoping I wasn't opening the door to something more sinister.

The doctor checked her watch and said, "I have rounds in five; I have to go. You still have my card?"

I nodded.

"Anything else happens, you call me—and I mean *call*, not simply appear."

I meant to smile at her but felt my lips press together to form a frown instead.

"You're scared—I get that—but you haven't been committing these murders. Maybe you *do* have terrible luck, but there are no such things as curses." She took a beat. "If a month goes by and your memories don't return, call me, and we can try hypnotherapy. Until then, try to live your life as best you can, Addison. I'm sure things will start to look up once you start remembering."

I nodded at her, and she left, taking her latte with her.

Well, that had been nothing more than a huge time suck. I'd gone to the doctor hoping to find answers, imagining she'd snap her fingers or use hypnosis to make me remember on the spot. Instead, I got open the door to let my memories in. If that vapour cloud from Stoker's was my memories personified, I feared it might bust the door down long before I let it in.

Piers had contacted the driver's family to let them know he'd pay for the funeral. He felt responsible for the man's life. "If I had not ordered him to drive you home that night…" he'd told me. I tried to console him, but it was to no avail. I hadn't seen Piers so distraught before. Granted, I hadn't known him for long in my current state, but he just didn't seem the type.

The funeral was a graveside service. Though I didn't really know the man, he *had* lost his life making sure I'd arrived safely home, and I felt I owed him at least that. I found the funeral party minutes before the service began and hung out on the periphery, feeling as if I didn't really belong.

"You made it," a voice whispered into my ear. I turned to see Piers' lackey, Percival, standing much too close for comfort.

I took a step forward and said, "Wouldn't have missed it for the world." I berated myself for sounding too jovial, given the circumstance of the occasion. "Since we're stating the obvious, I see you've made it, too."

"I worked with the guy, so…wouldn't have missed it for the world."

"A man is dead. This isn't a joking manner," I told him.

"Feeling a little responsible, are we?"

"A little," I admitted.

"I wonder, Addison: why is that?"

"He died in front of my condo. He died because he took me home."

"Truer words," he said. When I turned to look at him, he was grinning, as if he enjoyed taunting me.

The priest began the service. I looked up, looked around, and tried to put some distance between me and Percival, but he matched my every step.

"Piers isn't here," he said. "Strange, isn't it?"

"Maybe he's caught in traffic. He'll be here."

"Would it surprise you to learn he won't? It's overcast today, but he wouldn't chance it."

"Afraid of lightning, is he? Melting in the rain?"

"Something like that." He was standing sort of behind me so I couldn't see what he was doing, but I sensed him looking at me, his eyes sizing me up. "Piers told me he'd organized a moonlight vigil. He plans to attend that, instead."

I turned to him and whispered, "Aren't you afraid I'll tell Piers you're bothering me?" I didn't relish invoking Piers' name in vain, but he'd seemed beaten into submission with very few of Piers' words earlier.

Percival shrugged, feigning bravado, no doubt. "Tell me something, Lady Addison: would it surprise you to know you were more to blame than the acceptance of a lift home from the dead man would imply?"

A chill went down my spine; Percival had struck a nerve. "I don't know what you mean," I said, trying to sound calm.

"You've suspected it, haven't you? You've wondered why people around are dropping like flies."

I took another step away from him and into the crowd of mourners until I was standing with them, three rows deep. It wasn't the fact Percival had followed me that surprised me, but that he continued to dig.

"First, the barista; then, the bartender; now the driver…and those are just the ones we know about."

One of the mourners turned to shush him angrily.

"This is a funeral, Percival. Show some respect," I told him, surprised it actually worked. He remained silent through the rest of the service. So silent, in fact, I thought he'd left, but when I turned away from the plot, I saw him leaning against a tree in the distance.

"I can help," he told me after the service.

"If I ever need your help—and I won't—I'll be sure to ask."

"What you saw at Stoker's the other night wasn't fog from the DJ's machine. It wasn't a spectre, either."

I desperately wanted to ask what he was talking about. If it wasn't fog or a spectre, then what had it been? More importantly, how could I prevent its return? Instead, I walked away without another word.

We retired to Stoker's to drink to the driver. Piers picked up the tab. We sat in Piers' regular booth surrounded by many in his entourage, though Percival was noticeably absent.

I was on my second drink when I turned to Piers and asked, "What's Percy's deal?"

"Who?"

"Percival," I clarified. "What's his deal?"

Piers smiled. I may have misread it, but it looked like a nervous one. "I do not know what you mean."

"He approached me at the funeral today. Said he knew what happened to me at Stoker's when I thought I saw the spectre. Said he could help."

"Percival is...troubled," Piers said. "Not only that, he *is* trouble. You would be wise to stay away from him."

"If he's that much trouble, why keep him around?"

Piers' features grew angry. He let out what seemed like a growl as he focussed off into the distance. "You are absolutely right," he said, and he was off in a flash.

People on the dance floor parted. The crowd let out a series of audible gasps. Someone screamed.

I pushed my way through the crowd to see Percival at its centre. He was on the ground with Piers on top of him. For a moment, it looked as if Piers' mouth was on Percival's neck, but then I realized he was bent over him and whispering something in his ear. His hands were around Percival's neck.

"Stop, Piers!" I shouted, but Piers didn't budge.

"Piers," I said louder, approaching the men. When I put a hand on his shoulder, he shrugged me off. It was a simple, little gesture, but it sent me flying back into the crowd. Rather than prevent me from falling like in that trust-building exercise, people backed away from me, and I landed on my rump with a thud.

"Piers," I called from my position on the floor. "Enough!"

He either finally heard me or was finished throttling the man, because his back straightened. He stood up, pulled at his coattails, and rolled his shoulders. When he turned toward me, he seemed surprised to find me on the floor, and he held a hand out to help me up. Once I was on my feet, he embraced me and said, "We need to talk."

Percival remained on the floor. He'd been on his back while Piers had been on top of him. Now, he rolled onto his side and clutched his throat.

"But Percival…" I said. "He needs help."

"Percival will be fine. He will join us as soon as he is able." Piers sounded remarkably calm for a man that had just throttled an acquaintance within an inch of his life.

Piers led me to a door labelled "Staff Only" at the end of the bathroom corridor.

"What's going on?" I asked as Percival rounded the corner behind us.

"We have come to an agreement," Piers said. "We will hear him out and decide his fate later."

"Wait…decide his *fate*?"

Percival smiled to reveal a small welt just inside his mouth. A thin sheen of blood covered his teeth. I surmised he must've bit himself when he'd gone down after Piers had thrown him. "A fate worse than banishment," Percival said.

Piers seemed to sneer. "Let's get on with this explanation of yours, shall we?"

Percival unlocked the staff entrance.

"Wait…you work here?" I asked. "I thought you worked for Piers."

"The relationship is more complicated than that," Percival said.

"Complicated how?"

Percival turned to me and grinned, teeth still bloody. "You have no idea."

He led us down a long hallway, ending in a flight of stairs leading down.

"Wait," Piers said. He put a hand on my shoulder and spun me around to face him. "Think about this carefully. You might not want to know whatever is down there."

"She's going to learn the truth eventually, Piers—"

Piers turned on Percival, and I thought I might have to referee another fight. "That is enough from you," he said.

Percival opened his mouth as if to say more, but no sound came out.

Piers said, "Addison is not some…broken toy in need of repair." I put a hand on his back between his shoulder blades, feeling the tension there. Though his temper was on the verge of homicidal, it was sweet the way he wanted to protect me.

"It's okay, Piers. Whatever it is, I want to know…I *need* to know."

Piers nodded and told Percival, "Lead on, Macduff," and we descended the staircase.

There was another, long hallway at the base of it, dead-ending in another doorway. Percival unlocked that door, as well. It swung open onto a darkened room. I took Piers' hand, searching for moral support as I interlocked my fingers with his. He squeezed my hand to indicate he approved.

Nothing could have prepared me for when Percival switched on the lights. The "room" seemed to go on forever. Additional fluorescents glowed to life in sequence, revealing more and more of the structure. The only way I could describe what I was looking at would be to liken it to a library. The floor plan was in the shape of a square donut, with a railing around the centre "hole". When I looked over the edge, I counted three more floors below us. It was decorated in old-style, university library, down to the card catalogues opposite us. Wooden shelves lined the walls packed chock-full of ancient-looking books. A number of wooden tables had been set up at various points around the floor, sporting bankers' lamps with green glass shades.

"What…how…?" I started, unable to find the words.

"I urge you, Addison," Piers said, sounding frightened. It was a new emotion for him as far as I was concerned. "Do not do this."

"Do what?" I asked.

"She'll discover your involvement in the whole sordid affair soon enough, Piers. Don't you think it better to rip the bandage off quickly?"

"Mark my words: I *will* kill you when this is done," Piers warned. Judging by his tone of voice, I fully believed he would.

"Piers!" I said. "This is *my* life. Don't you understand? People are dying. I need to know if I had anything to do with their deaths."

"Wise girl," Percival said.

"Do not—"

"Enough, Piers," I said. I turned to Percival and asked, "What *is* this place?"

"We call it the Library, but technically, it's probably more of an archive."

"Why build it under Stoker's?"

Piers grunted his disapproval, pulled a chair from the nearest table, and more slouched than sat in it.

"The Library pre-dates Stoker's by some hundred years or so. It was my idea to turn the storefront into a Goth club to attract the interesting patronage."

"So, *you* own this place?"

"Not me, personally. The name on the lease is the Curatorial Foundation. I'm just the current custodian of the property."

"The Curatorial Foundation?" I asked.

"Tread lightly, boy," Piers warned.

Percival motioned for us to take a seat at the same table as Piers on the opposite side. "I'm what's known as a curator—"

"More like a glorified librarian," Piers said, pouting.

Percival glared at Piers.

"What sorts of things do you curate?" I asked.

"The long answer? The term, 'curator' comes from the Medieval Latin '*curitas*', its root meaning 'spiritual oversight', one responsible for the cure of souls. The short answer is that I curate information about stuff similar to what you're experiencing."

"The girl at the Pumpkin Spice said something about a curse. Does my soul need some sort of cure for that?"

"In a word: yes."

I turned to Piers. "Did you know about this?"

He looked at Percival as if warning him not to contradict him again. "I am aware, yes," Piers said.

"And the girl at the Pumpkin Spice—Percival...you knew she was tied up in this, too?"

Piers nodded. "As was Persephone, yes."

Seph, too? These people purported to love me. Now I'd learned everything they'd said to me in recent memory had been a lie.

"Is there anything else you'd like to tell me?" I asked Piers. I felt the blood heat in my veins. My face flushed. Ever since I'd met...*re*-met Piers and Seph, I'd been nothing short of one millimetre from frightening my pants off. In a way, it was refreshing to experience something as primal and visceral as anger instead.

"Think carefully before answering, Piers. Wouldn't want to wake the beast within before we're ready, now, would we?" It was an odd turn of phrase, but I chalked it up to Percival's awkward show of bluster. Being smarmy to Piers must have been as refreshing a release for Percival as was anger for me.

Piers glared at Percival and said through clenched teeth, "Listen to what the man has to say."

"Go on, Percival," I prompted.

He held a finger up, stood, and disappeared into the stacks.

Obviously still fuming, Piers said, "We could go now. Leave before he returns. We could leave the city, too, never to return. I do not know what he is about to say, but I promise you: you will not be happy with whatever it is he has discovered."

The centre of the structure acted as an echo chamber, and we heard Percival's return seconds before we saw him emerge from between the stacks, carrying a huge, hardcover book. "Near as I can figure, you have a tulpa."

"A what?"

"A tulpa: an intelligent companion imagined into existence."

I turned to Piers and asked, "What was I into before I lost my memories? I mean, an all-black wardrobe, Goth clubs, occult shops, safe houses…"

Piers opened his mouth as if to speak, but I cut him off. "The truth, this time." He just shrugged and shook his head.

"Ordinarily," Percival continued, his nose buried in the book as he tried to find the page he was looking for, "tulpas aren't malicious unless you mess up during the creation process—"

"What does this have to do with the barista?"

Percival looked up from the book. "Quite frankly, she messed up."

"So, I was *trying* to create a tulpa and went to her for help?" I gasped when realization dawned. "Is that what killed those people?"

"Can you not see you are freaking her out?" Piers said. "Let us take a step back. You were not trying to create a tulpa. I think what Percival is trying to say is that the tulpa was inadvertently created when the barista screwed up."

"Why would I have gone to her in the first place?" The anger I'd felt earlier had morphed into something half-way between fear and panic. If I'd created the tulpa, if the tulpa was mine, it meant I was inadvertently responsible for at least three deaths that I knew of.

Piers sat up in his chair and continued, "The Pumpkin Spice usually employs witches with wicked skills." He paused as if considering his words. "To be clear: wickedly good at casting spells—*good* spells—not wicked ones."

"Spells?" The notion that magick was real, that someone could cast an actual spell to act upon another human being was the domain of the fantastic—wasn't it?

"The barista, as you call her, on duty that day was more of a novice."

"Why would she go ahead with the…spell if she couldn't do it properly?" The correct answer to that question was: because she knew she was perpetrating a scam, and she wanted the money. I wasn't prepared for Percival's actual answer.

"Because she was arrogant?" he said. "Kids come to the big city for university from all points Hicksville, Ontario and beyond. They watch too much television, climb out of mommy and daddy's helicopter, and think it's fun to dabble in the occult. My guess is that the barista was a novice wanna-be given the keys to the shop, and she decided to be Ferris Bueller for the day. Unfortunately, your tulpa is Cameron's dad's car."

Percival continued flipping pages. When he found the one he'd been looking for, he put his pointer finger down in the centre of it and said, "Aha! Here it is. I call this volume *Tulpamancy for Dummies.*

"It says here, tulpas are 'creatures of the mind', controlled hallucinations created by people who have reality-warping powers and nurtured over years if not decades. They exist in an imaginary setting created by the tulpamancer in his or her mind—"

I thought of the face I'd seen in the vapour trail at the club. "Why would anyone intentionally want to hallucinate?" I glanced over at Piers, but he remained silent, his face expressionless.

Percival answered my question with another question; I hated that. "Why do people take drugs?"

"Point taken."

"Maybe they're lonely?" he continued. "When one imagines such a creature into existence, they eventually become as real to the tulpamancer as an imaginary friend is to a child.

"At first, one must think for the tulpa, but over time, the tulpa seems to take on a life of its own, becoming capable of playing the part of a real person in the mind of its creator, eventually freeing itself of its maker's control. That's where the process wades into dangerous waters."

Percival flipped a page so brittle, I thought it might crumble in his hands. "According to this, there's no real proof tulpas are able to manifest physically or that they possess supernatural abilities, other than some cautionary tales to would-be tulpamancers, the sources of which are unverifiable. It also says tulpas can be dangerous if they manifest in a particularly disturbed, angry, or fearful mind.

"I'd say that was you to a T, my dear."

That didn't sound like me. Fearful? Yes, ever since my amnesia had taken hold. Disturbed? Maybe, considering the fact that people were dropping dead around me and I couldn't remember who I was. Angry? Not until I'd climbed down Percival's rabbit hole. I hated being with people who knew more about me than I did.

"Percival!" Piers bellowed. "Enough glib."

Percival gave a flourish and mock-bowed. "As you wish, Master."

Piers glowered at him.

"Why would I go to a witch to help me create a tulpa, of all things?"

"Imposition," Percival said.

I furrowed my brow at him to indicate I had no idea what he'd meant.

"Imposition is the process of using your senses to imagine a tulpa into being. The correct question is: why would you go to a witch to help with the imposition of a tulpa? The answer is: you didn't. The tulpa was created through her ineptitude."

It explained a lot. If whatever I had done with the girl at the Pumpkin Spice had been botched and created a tulpa, it would explain why I'd felt the vapour's sentience when it had circled me. Rather than my creating memories with the tulpa through life-experience, maybe the tulpa had stolen my memories when it manifested. It would also explain why I'd experienced that moment of crystal clarity when it had jumped me.

"The correct question is," Percival continued, "why would you have need for the services of a witch in the first place?"

"And the answer?" I asked.

"Want to field this one, Piers?"

Piers grumbled something unintelligible, leaned forward in his chair, and said, "You went there for a cure of sorts."

"So, I *was* cursed."

"Not exactly," Piers said.

"Let's say you were," Percival interjected, "for the sake of argument. Any thoughts as to who might have cursed you?" He paused before saying, "Piers?"

If looks could kill, Percival would have been dead ten times over. "I *will* kill you for this," Piers warned Percival, "slow and painfully over all of eternity." Piers certainly had a flair for hyperbole.

"I regret to inform it was I. Your situation, the one that drove you to find a witch, is on me. I cursed you. Persephone, too, if it matters."

"What do you mean it was you?"

"I had no other choice. You hated what you had become. I felt responsible—"

"Damn right you were responsible. If you loved me as much as you said, why would you curse me in the first place?"

"You begged me. From the moment you learned what I was. When I told you I would have to eventually leave because of it, you pleaded for me to turn you—"

"Into what?" I asked.

"Into something I would not wish upon my worst enemy." Piers paused as if to gauge my reaction.

"But you did it anyway—"

"You wanted it. I would not have turned you if you had not asked. I would never turn anyone unless they asked."

"Huh," I said. "And Seph?"

116

"She said she could not live without you.

"You were okay with what you had become for many years, but our way of life eventually took its toll, and you grew despondent, suicidal, talked about ending it all.

"I had known about Percival's...legacy," he held his arms out and looked up at the ceiling as if to indicate the library in its entirety, "and I asked if he could help. You agreed to wait until we had an answer."

"We spent weeks...months poring over every ancient document, every book, every scroll, every online source we could find, including those in the far recesses of the Dark Web where age-old sorcerers are said to dwell, until, at last, we found a cure," Percival explained.

"The magick needed was powerful, and the person executing the spell had to be as powerful. My sources on the Dark Web pointed me toward the Pumpkin Spice. The owner is said to practice old magick, like inquisition and Salem Witch Trials powerful—"

"The barista claimed to have been the owner," Piers continued. "She said she could perform the spell which ultimately cleft you in two: Addison, the new you, and Prudence, the old you, the one I have loved for all of these years."

Prudence—the one he'd loved. I felt thrown for a loop. Betrayed, yet again. "You made love to *me*. *You* initiated intimacy. Were you thinking of her while you were with me?" I asked.

"It is not like that," he defended.

"Why don't you tell me what it *is* like?"

"There is more of Prudence in you than there is you in Prudence—"

I held my hands out, palms up, and looked away from him. "I don't even know what that means."

"It means that I see more similarities between you and her than differences. As much as I love her, I am drawn to *you*."

"You smell her humanity," Percival interjected. I'd almost forgotten he was there.

Piers turned on him, closing the distance between them in an instant. "From this moment forward," he growled, "you will speak when spoken to. Understood?"

Percival cowered. "Yes, sir."

The momentum of our argument lost, I asked, "She's dangerous, isn't she; my tulpa?"

Piers nodded.

Percival put his hand up, asking for the opportunity to speak. Piers sighed and said, "Yes, Percival?" sounding frustrated.

"Technically what you have isn't a tulpa, not exactly, but it's the closest analogy we could find in the research."

"That's not helpful," I told him.

I was neither Prudence nor Addison; I had neither tulpa nor spectre; I had either been cursed or turned; I had most certainly been conned by that barista and was starting to wonder if Piers and Percival weren't doing the same. Exactly what had I given up to be with Piers? What could I have possibly to make me desperate enough to let a total stranger cast a spell on me with ancient and powerful magick?

Tulpas, spectres, curses, witches, spells, magick...

The air around me grew soupy, thickening with every second ticking by until I could no longer breathe. "I need some air," I told the men, and I rushed toward the door.

118

"It is a lot to take in," Piers said. I think he'd meant for it to have been sympathetic, but the darkness had begun to close in, and I wasn't in the mood for the warm fuzzies.

"I need some time." I reached for the doorknob, but Percival called to me staying my hand.

"Of course, you do," Percival said, fraught with more condescension than empathy, "but don't take too long. Humans you interact with tend to wind up eaten. Speaking on behalf of myself, that nice doctor you spoke to, and most of the city's population, I'd like to keep my jugular intact."

Percival's phone buzzed. "Saved by the bell," he said. He glanced at it. "911…literally. The police are here. They want to question us about your driver's death."

Stoker's was abuzz with police activity. Two men wearing dark trench coats and dark suits were sitting at a table waiting for us. They stood as we approached. The taller of the two was the first to hold a hand out to us. "This must be the famed Addison Haney I've heard so much about of late," he said. I glanced at the badge on his lapel and the gun in his holster. "Detective Constable Jay Harker," he told me. We shook hands. "I'd like to speak with you, if I may." He motioned back to his partner who was still standing.

"Of course." I went over to sit at the table along with Piers and Harker. "Detective Constable Kevin Reeves," Harker said, introducing his partner.

"In what capacity did you know the deceased?" Reeves asked once I'd gotten comfortable in my chair.

"He was Piers' driver. He drove me home three times," I said.

"How *well* did you know the deceased?"

About as well as I know myself, I wanted to say. "I didn't know him at all. He sat in the front of the car, I sat in the back."

"When was the last time you saw him?"

"He dropped me off in front of my building last night, and I went upstairs to bed. I made my morning coffee, looked down through my window, saw the commotion, and went outside to investigate."

Harker looked up as Seph came into the club.

"Hail, hail, the gang's all here," Reeves said. "Miss Underwood, so nice of you to join us." He held a hand out for her to shake. Reeves was turning out to be a snarky little bugger. "Please." He motioned at an empty chair.

"What's this about?" Seph asked me.

"Uh-uh-uh," Reeves said. "Me and Harker," he made a fist, extended the thumb as if he were about to hitchhike, and used it to point at his partner, "will ask all of the questions, if you don't mind."

Seph nodded. She looked at me, opening her eyes wide and raising her eyebrows as if to ask what that guy's problem was.

"We were just talking about the driver's death. Where were you on the night in question, Miss Underwood?" Harker asked.

"I was at home," she said.

"Can anyone corroborate your alibi?"

Seph paused before saying, "I was at home with my… girlfriend."

I turned to look at her head on. "You have a girlfriend?"

Seph shrugged.

"Here you are, flirting with me like you want to get back together, and you had a girlfriend all along?"

Reeves rapped on the table twice. "Can we focus, people, please?"

Harker continued the interrogation. "You three seem pretty cozy, Mr. Westenra—"

"Piers, please," Piers interrupted.

"How are you, Miss Haney, and Mr...Stoker, was it—acquainted?

"We are friends," Piers said.

"Care to elaborate on the relationship, Miss Haney?"

Piers glared at me with a warning expression. "Pervical came on to me. Piers was jealous. We thought it best to have a discussion with Percival letting him know the unwanted attention needed to stop."

Harker turned to Percival and said, "Anything to add, Mr. Stoker?"

Percival shrugged. "I'm a beast. I see what I want, and I go after it."

It was enough to make my whole body shudder. If Percival *were* a beast, it was one oozing stinky slime.

Reeves handed Harker an iPad. Harker lifted the cover, flipped the tablet around, and slid it over on the table to show me a picture of myself and the driver. I was wearing a short, black, leather skirt, a red, double-breasted, leather jacket, and stilettos, my arm crooked around the driver's. He reached across the table, slid left on the iPad, and revealed another image taken on the same night. This time, the driver was leaning against the wall of a building in a laneway, and my face was buried in the juncture between his shoulder and his neck. Harker slid left again to an image of what looked like me macking down on the driver's elbow-pit.

"Let me ask you again," Harker said. "How well did you know the deceased?"

"My girl was in an accident," Piers explained. "She has amnesia."

"First Percy, then the ex, now the driver," Reeves summed. He made a fist and pointed in my direction with the same outstretched thumb as before. "Got your hands full with this one, don'tcha?"

"A little respect, please," Piers warned.

Reeves shrugged. "I'm just sayin'…"

Piers closed his eyes and planted his hands on the table in front of him as if he were trying to summon strength and solemnity. "What we do or do not do in our relationships is none of your concern."

"So, it's that way, is it?" Reeves said.

"See, that's where you're wrong, I'm afraid," Harker jumped in. "Once your buddy turned up dead, what you do or do not do in your relationships is *exactly* my concern."

"Addison did not know my driver other than when he drove her home," Piers reiterated.

"These pictures would seem to say otherwise," Harker said.

Piers shrugged and leaned back in his seat.

"Miss Haney?" Harker asked.

I looked at Piers, turned my head just enough to see Seph in my peripheral vision, turned back to the detectives, and shrugged. "Like Piers said: I have amnesia."

"Do you deny that's you in the photographs?"

I didn't know how long I'd be able to maintain my composure. There was no denying it was me in the pictures. There was also no denying it appeared as if I'd known the driver before giving birth to my tulpa, and intimately so. Piers seemed to have known about the relationship. What was even more puzzling was that given the heat between us and the fact he claimed to love me, he seemed to be okay with my dalliance with the driver.

"It certainly looks like me, but I have no recollection of the events they depict."

"Convenient," Reeves said. I wondered if he'd volunteered to play bad cop to Harker's good cop before they'd arrived, or if he had a naturally lousy disposition.

Harker touched the tablet screen and used his fingers to zoom in on the image where my mouth had settled on the delicate skin of the driver's inner elbow.

More unsettling than the fact Piers seemed okay with my intimacy with the driver was seeing myself with him in the images, given the strong attraction I had for Piers. Considering my feelings for Piers, how could I have found myself in such a compromising situation with another man?

"Care to comment?" Harker said.

"What, exactly, am I supposed to be looking at?" I asked.

"Unless I'm mistaken, that," he pointed to the tablet, "is blood."

The image wouldn't allow for any further enlargement, so I brought the tablet closer to my face. "Or it could be lipstick," I offered.

Piers leaned toward me to take a closer look for himself. "Could be lipstick," he confirmed.

Reeves huffed. Harker frowned.

Piers took the tablet from my hands and showed it to Percival."Lipstick," Percival said after examining the close-up. "I concur."

"If I were either of you, I wouldn't get too smart," Reeves warned. He turned to Piers and said, "The way I see it, the driver was playing with your girl-toy," he turned to Percival, "which also happened to be the object of *your* desire."

"I'm sitting right here, you misogynist pig," I told Reeves.

"Calling a cop a pig—how original," Reeves said, deadpan.

"And don't you get too comfortable either, missy," he told Seph. "I haven't quite figured out how you fit into all of this, but you seem to have your eyes on the exact same prize."

"Am I under arrest?" I asked. Seph booted me under the table. Piers glared. Percival smiled as if the entertainment for the night was just getting started.

Harker looked at Reeves who shrugged.

Piers said, "Look, officers, we have a lot to discuss—"

"I'll *bet* you do," Reeves interrupted.

"If you're done with the interrogation..."

"Are we done, Harker?"

Harker picked the tablet up and closed the cover. "Yeah," he said standing. "We're done...for now."

Reeves stood and said, "Don't even think about leaving town before the investigation's over. As far as I'm concerned, you're all suspects in this case. The only question I have is if someone's individually responsible, or whether you offed the guy as a group." One thing could be said for Reeves: the guy didn't mince words.

I shuddered again. Though I might have been indirectly and individually responsible for the driver's death, the group was collectively responsible for the cover-up.

When we were sure the police had left, Percival said, "I think I can find a solution for you. Give me a day or so."

"A solution?" Seph asked. "To what?"

"To Addison's…situation," Piers said.

"Is that what you want, sweetie?" Seph asked.

"When were you going to tell me you had a girlfriend?" It was stupid to feel jealous, I know, but I felt an undeniable connection, a…pull, if you will, toward Seph that was every bit as strong as the one I felt for Piers. What had Piers said earlier? That he'd turned both Seph and myself when we'd asked? The unanswered question remaining on my lips was: turned into what?

Seph shrugged. "If and when the time presented itself."

"When was that going to be?"

"Probably never, since the moment you lost your memory you turned to the gigolo instead of me—"

"Piers is…" I had the impulse to defend him, but I couldn't think of how. If he truly was the one responsible for whatever the barista had done to me, then he was also indirectly responsible for connecting me—or rather, a part of me—to the murders happening around me.

"Ladies, please," Percival interjected. "Can we focus?"

The show obviously over, Piers approached me, put his hands on my biceps and squeezed gently. "If you are truly unhappy with me as a partner, if you would rather be with Persephone, just say the word, and I will release you from our bond."

"We have a bond?" Things just kept getting better.

To recap: I used to be intimate with Seph; Piers had turned me into…God only knew what; the procedure to undo whatever he had done to me was botched; I had a tulpa going around killing people; the police had photographs of me and the driver making out before the barista…unturned me, for lack of a better term; and Percival was a curator, someone who hoarded resources on the supernatural. And if those revelations weren't mind-boggling enough, I'd slept with Piers because we had some kind of bewitching, binding bond between us.

Wonderful!

I took a breath in, but nothing came. I tried again—still nothing. The atmosphere in the bar turned boggy, and I began to hyperventilate. "I need some air," I managed between gasps, and made a beeline for the door.

Outside, the sun beat down on me, its heating rays interrupted by a slight breeze, and my lungs began to open up again. I leaned my forehead against a column holding up the portico just outside the entrance.

The door behind me whooshed open. I turned to see Piers standing just inside the doorway. "Addison, please come back in. We need to talk."

"What *am* I?" I asked him, my forehead still against the cool stone of the column.

"You are...human." The very sound of the word seemed to pain him.

"And what are you?"

"What I am is complicated to explain—"

"Uncomplicate it for me."

"I am...something else."

I stood up straight and looked at him. Though I'd heard enough crazy stuff over the last few days, I hesitated to believe him. The question remained: if he was something other than human, what exactly was he? And by extension: what was Seph? What had *I* been before my incident at the Pumpkin Spice?

"Well," I said. My shirt had ridden up during my panic attack, and I smoothed it, pulling it down so it covered the small of my back. "Thank you for having enough respect for me to tell me the truth," I told him, unsure if he would get the sarcasm, and walked away.

I noticed Piers didn't follow. "Where are you going?" he called to me from inside the bar.

"Anywhere but here." I didn't know if I'd said it loudly enough for him to hear, and I wasn't sure I cared.

"Percival—I need you," I heard Piers call, but either Percival wasn't available to coax me back, or he knew enough to respect my privacy, because to my knowledge, no one followed me.

Dr. Putnum had suggested I try visualization to confront my former self in an attempt to reunite us. I thought I might try it to initiate communication, maybe talk her into leaving me for good. Whatever Piers and Seph were, I wanted no part of it.

I looked around my condo. It was a significant size, considering some of the newer waterfront units, on the penthouse floor, and in a prime location. Given the real estate boom in the city, I might be able to get a few million on the market if I acted fast. A million dollars would be more than enough to buy a ticket to points outside the Americas and lose myself forever. If I could only convince my tulpa to stay behind, I could cut bonds and grow old after making a new life for myself.

The irony that I was in my situation because I'd already tried to make a new life for myself wasn't lost on me.

Tulpa first. Pulling up stakes later. One problem at a time.

If my tulpa were as dangerous as she seemed, if she liked eating humans, I'd need some protection against her. Though I didn't think she'd be hungry enough to eat *me*—technically, she and I were one and the same—I figured I'd be better off safe than sorry.

I googled "protection against spirits". In addition to invoking Jesus' name and holy water, blessed salt and rosaries were supposed to help. A search of my jewelry collection came up empty for rosaries. I did, however, find an ancient-looking amulet with an ankh on it and decided to put it on, figuring it couldn't hurt. While I had no access to holy water, I had no problem praying before I began the visualization process. I knew I had a one-kilogram bag of salt in my kitchen cupboard, and I went to get it. There was a bag of tea lights in one of the kitchen drawers, and I took that, too, figuring it would help set the mood. I found a book of matches in the drawer with which to light the candles.

Back in my living room, I held the bag of salt in my arms. "I bless this salt in Jesus' name," I said, hoping it was enough, and poured it out in the shape of a large circle. I set the tea lights around the outside perimeter of the salt circle and lit them. When I was done, I turned the lights off and sat cross-legged in the centre of the salt circle.

"Prudence?" I said, closing my eyes. My hands rested on my knees, palms up, in a sort of Lotus Pose. "I call on you, Prudence." The air grew noticeably cooler, and I sensed I was no longer alone. I opened my eyes, expecting to see my breath and saw a thin mist materializing in the corner of the room instead.

"Prudence, is that you?" The mist thickened to a fog. As I watched, the puff of fog grew to a cloud and gradually spread across the room in my direction. It neared me, seeming to speed up as if to rush me. Though it had no face, it appeared to grimace in pain when it hit the edge of the salt circle, as if there were an invisible pillar force field around me through which it was unable to penetrate.

The cloud dissipated and then grew thick again. I looked into the centre of the vapour to see what looked like my face reflected back, only with a different expression than mine. While my jaw felt lax, my eyebrows raised, and my eyes open wider than usual, the features of my reflection were taut, her lips pursed in a thin frown, and her eyebrows knit together. Her eyes narrowed, and it dawned on me that I wasn't looking at my face in a reflection, but upon that of my tulpa.

And she was pissed.

Not in the mood to mince words, I asked, "What do you want?" but there was no response.

"You're ruining my life," I told her.

What makes you think it is your life to ruin? The answer came to me in my mind, and I wondered if I hadn't answered myself for a moment. *Perhaps you are the one that has ruined* my *life with your little stunt.*

"Correct me if I'm wrong, but you were the one to trust that barista in the first place. This is what *you* wanted. I didn't exist until *you* messed up."

You existed. You have always existed, came the answer. *You are me before I met Piers. You are the one who begged to be with him for all of eternity. You had no life before I came along, and do not forget it.*

What she'd said made sense—Addison Haney *was* an alias Prudence had concocted in advance of her exit, after all.

"If your life was so great, why did you want to change it?"

Piers told me I would have great hunger after the change, and that I had to control it until he could provide for me. When I awoke, the need was too great. Piers was nowhere to be found, so I set out in search of food on my own. I drained four people that night, an entire family including two children, before the self-loathing set in.

She showed me an image of myself covered in blood that wasn't my own. The rest of her story unfolded as if I were watching a movie in my mind. I wandered from the hovel and into the cobblestone street, leaving the bodies of my victims behind. Piers happened upon me a few minutes later and brought me back to his abode, a brick row-house a few streets over.

Piers explained that he could supply me with the blood I needed to survive if only I was able to fight the hunger. He also told me it would have been easier to control the cravings had I waited for him to return.

She spoke her next words in unison with the image of Piers in my mind: "Once you have tasted blood from the source, from a living, beating heart, you will crave it until the end of time.

"But you are strong, Pru, my dear. I have faith you will learn to control the hunger in time."

I managed to control the hunger for more than a century, but something changed. Re-warmed blood from a bag no longer sated, so I struck out. There were reports of cougar-sightings within the city limits, and I used them to my advantage, exacting a little more damage than usual so the authorities would think the animal at fault, but when the hunger returned, so, too, did the guilt.

I hoped she wouldn't show me images of her most recent victims.

Percival retreated to his little library in an attempt to find a reason for the increase in bloodlust. Other than as a reaction to a recent eclipse or change in the earth's atmosphere, he had no explanation. That whole archive, four floors of books, journals, and whatnot, not to mention the entire of the Dark Web, and he could find no explanation.

He did, however, learn of a cure, which brings us to the present.

"Why do you continue to haunt me?"

Haunt you? Have you not heard a word I have said? My bloodlust has returned tenfold, and I must feed. You may have stolen my body, but I am still tied to you. I have no choice but to "haunt" you, as you say. You and I are one and the same. We will be until the end of time.

"So, there's no getting rid of you." My heart grew heavy. I felt my shoulders droop and tears burn as they formed in my eyes.

My getting rid of you has been liberating, she said. *You, Addison Haney, are my guilt personified. I satisfy my cravings, and you assume all the blame. It seems to me the only way to rid yourself of me is to break the ties that bind.*

"How would I go about that? The ancient witch is long dead. So is the barista. The only one who could perform any sort of ritual—"

Is Percival.

"If he could perform rituals, why send me to the Pumpkin Spice?"

Percival has no inherent magick with which to perform spells. He can do it, but there is no more than a fifty-fifty chance it will stick.

"No better than the barista."

It is, at least, a chance. He does, however, possess the passion needed in order to make the spell work. Piers and his influence aside, the police presence at Stoker's cannot be good for business.

I thought about her proposal: to wait for Percival to find a solution to my problem, a way to separate Prudence and I for all eternity. On the flip-side, it also meant finding a way to release a supernatural killer into the world, one that killed without remorse. Not to mention it would wear my face while doing so.

Before I could protest, Prudence said, *There is one solution: break the salt circle. Let me in. We can become one again,* as if reading my mind, which I suppose she probably could.

"One killing machine," I said.

I swear on my life—on our lives—to curb my cravings. I will behave myself, and you can break your cycle of self-loathing.

Could I trust her? Rather, could I trust myself? Hadn't I tried to resist the pull Piers had on me and failed? Hadn't I tried to ignore the feelings I had for Seph and still felt jealous when I learned she had a girlfriend?

"If I agree to this, I will hold you to your word. If you kill anything as large as a fly, I will find a way to end us *both* next time."

Agreed, she said.

I nodded my affirmation. "What now?" I asked.

Break the salt circle.

I reached out and brushed a path through the line of salt with the side of my hand.

Brace yourself, Pru said.

"Will it hurt?"

Physically, no, but mentally it will feel as though you are in the throes of the world's worst hangover.

Ready?

I nodded again. "Ready."

Prudence retreated, her misty body swirling and curling in the dark. She turned, and I fancied I could see her face drawn in the vapour, smiling.

I took in a breath to tell her I'd made a mistake, that what we were planning to do was wrong, and that we should wait for Percival to figure it out like he'd promised, but it was too late. She advanced on me once more, penetrating what was left of the salt circle with ease to envelop me in her nebula. I felt her inside my body and inside my brain. I could hear her thoughts which seemed nothing more than a menacing laugh, and I steeled every muscle in my body against her.

Pru backed a few metres away from me, spun to form a tornado-like helix, and charged me again at full force. Once more, I felt her inside my brain, performing a Vulcan mind-meld as I shivered against her cold vapour, my teeth chattering.

When next she backed away, I fell backward onto the hardwood floor. My head hit the wood with a thud, and my body bridged what remained of the salt circle. I reached up to feel the base of my skull, expecting it to come away bloody; I wasn't disappointed.

Though Prudence said nothing—she didn't have to, given the way we were linked—the fact that I excited her to no end.

"Cool your jets, bitch," I told her. "If you feed on me there's nowhere left for you to go but down."

Pru swore.

"What now?" I asked.

It worked. I could feel it working. If you hadn't clenched your body against me—

"We're in this predicament because we used magick— maybe we need to use magick to get us out."

Getting Percival to magick me to Hell isn't an option. I thought we were in agreement—

I'd felt Pru's hunger when she was inside my head. The only way I could describe the bloodlust was to imagine my fiercest carb craving and multiply it infinity-fold. So intense was the hunger, I visualized myself ripping through the wall to the unit next-door and gorging on whatever I might find there. The thought was gloriously satisfying and wickedly frightening.

"Maybe I've changed my mind. The whole reason for us to join was to stop you from killing, but after melding with you, I'm not sure I'd be able to control myself. *You* certainly couldn't."

Pru continued to move in helictical fashion in front of me, her mist waxing and waning in translucence as if she were breathing. *Alone, we might not, but together, if we cooperate, we should be able to hold firm.*

"Might…if…should…your argument's not very convincing."

If you still need…convincing, as you say, even after all you claim to have experienced, there is a store of evidence for you to see.

"Evidence?"

I believe you have already found the safety deposit key? You will find all of the evidence you need inside that box.

"How can I use the key when I don't even know—" I stopped mid-sentence when Pru enveloped me in her frigid haze. The bank and the branch came to me as if she had whispered it in my ear.

Go to the bank. Use the key. All will be revealed.

The address Pru gave me was the same branch from which my condo fee payments were drawn. Though the bank machines were surprisingly empty, there *was* a long line-up—composed mostly of the middle-aged and the elderly—to see the tellers. Rather than wait in line, I went to the receptionist and asked about accessing my safety deposit box. She sent me to a cubicle on the far side of the establishment, where a young man was checking Instagram on his cell phone.

"Excuse me?" I said. The man looked up and blushed as if he'd been caught with his metaphoric pants down. I held the safety deposit key up for him to see.

"Ah," the man said with a nod. He bounded to his feet, opened the top desk drawer, dropped his phone into it, and fumbled to withdraw a ring of keys. "Number?"

I felt my mouth drop and my shoulders droop.

"That's okay," he said, reading my reaction. "I can find it for you. Name?"

That was a very good question. "Addison Haney," I said, hoping I'd make the right choice, seeing as how I didn't catch Prudence's last name.

The man went back to his office, tapped on his keyboard, came back, and said, "Six-Six-Six."

"I'm sorry?"

"Your safety deposit number. It's an easy one to remember, really." It was apt, too. Given the recent turn of events, I wondered if I'd asked for that particular number, or if it had been assigned through happenstance.

I thanked the man and followed him to the vault. Inside, small doors covered the façade of every wall like miniature refrigeration tanks in a morgue. Each door had two keyholes. He put his key into one of the holes, turned, and motioned for me to do the same with mine. Once unlocked, he swung the door open and removed a long, narrow, metal box which he took to a small, closet-like space containing a table and two chairs. He put the box on the table and said, "Let me know when you're done," and left the room, closing the door behind him.

There was another lock on the metal box, opened by my key. Inside the box were a series of photographs and clipped newspaper articles.

The first photo I picked up was sepia-toned, depicting Piers, myself, and Seph, dressed up like in those old-style photos you take at carnivals. Piers was wearing a dark suit with narrow lapels and a string tie. He looked quite dapper, even with his hair parted awkwardly in the centre and held in place with what looked like really greasy product. I was wearing a dark-coloured, Victorian dress, complete with corset, bustle, and parasol, my hair tied back in a low bun. Seph was similarly dressed, only her dress was lighter in colour than mine.

I saw my breath when I sighed; my first indication Pru was there with me.

"You're here," I said.

I thought you might need a bit of moral support. She materialized in front of me, a thin mist as a gauzy as my breath.

"This photo—"

It is not what you think.

"How do you know what I think?"

I am not prying, she said. *We are linked. I hear things.*

139

It is *authentic, in case you are wondering.*

"It can't be."

It can. It is.

"So I was born—"

1865. The child of farmers Elmer and Agnes, first-generation Canadians. Piers was born about fifty years earlier. His father was a former slave who escaped to Upper Canada using the Underground Railroad. His mother was a white British expat.

"And Seph?"

A city girl. I met her when I went to work in a dress shop on Lot Street—that is today's Queen Street—in the city of York. She came in to buy a dress. Most of the girls and women who shopped there were snobs, but not Seph. We became great friends and then something...more.

It felt as if I were living my own rendition of *Vampire Diaries*, unable to choose between bad boy Piers and Seph, the girl who had given up her human life to be with me through all of eternity. I put the photo down.

"Moving on..." I said, picking up the first news clipping I found. It was an article from *The Globe and Mail*, dated to 1886, the story of a series of animal attacks just north of the city. The deaths were attributed to a pack of wolves after passersby saw them feeding off one of the corpses.

I am not sure whether I saved those articles as a point of pride or hubris, Pru admitted, *but I kept them; all of them. It probably had something to do with the fact I had to live my life in the shadows, unable to lay claim to my fifteen minutes of fame.*

"Save the pop-psychology, why don't you?" I put the article down and moved the others around on the table. There were clippings from virtually every decade up until the late 1910s. The next article after that dated to only a few months ago. "What happened? Why did the articles stop?"

Blood transfusions gained popularity, making it easier for us to get blood.

"What did you do before then?"

Human donors. Most of them willing, but some of them...well, you can read for yourself.

"And then recently—"

I fell off the wagon. Her nonchalance was frightening.

There was a knock at the door, and it opened a crack. "I'm sorry, Miss Haney, but someone else is waiting for the room," the man said.

"I'll be just a minute," I told him. He closed the door, and I gathered up all of the articles and photographs, pausing when one of the images caught my eye. It was a picture of Piers wearing a tuxedo with me standing beside him, wearing a wedding gown and veil and holding a bouquet of flowers. Judging by the style of the dress and the quality of the photograph, it had been taken in the 1960s or '70s.

"What's this?" I asked Pru.

Relax, she said. *Before you go all weepy on me, that was taken at a Halloween party.*

"So we're not married?"

You sound disappointed.

"I'm not. I'm just...curious."

Piers and I toyed with the idea of getting married before I knew his secret, but given his...heritage, no one would perform the ceremony.

"But his parents—"

Were not married. They lived their lives as pariahs, isolated from the mainstream.

"How sad."

Sad does not begin to describe it.

There was another knock on the door. I collected the remaining documents, slid them into my purse, closed the safety deposit box, locked it, and left to return it to the vault.

I needed privacy.

Back in my condo bedroom, I poured salt across the doorjamb and in front of the sliding doors leading to the balcony. I also drew a large circle in front of my bed for good measure—my own Fortress of Solitude. Having dumped the collection from the safety deposit box in the centre of the circle, I grabbed my cell phone, entered the circle, and sat down.

What Pru had said at the bank was true (I googled it): blood collection was in full swing in Canada by 1910. It was collected in small, glass vials and proved a boon for the war effort, although indirect blood transfer, where it wasn't person-to-person before the blood coagulated, didn't happen until the thirties. Shortly after that, blood banks were established in North America in time for World War Two, which meant that at some point in time, the only way people like myself, Piers, and Seph could eat was if we had live donors. It also meant one of two things: either we had willing participants, or we took what we needed, as Pru had happened with the family she'd decimated.

Once put in chronological order, the news articles lent credence to Pru's story. There was a rash of animal killings in the City of York (what the city had been called before it was dubbed Toronto), spurred by reports from eye-witnesses of packs of animals—mostly wolves—feasting on the remains of human bodies. Reports of human-like beings with glowing eyes and long teeth similarly feasting had been reported, but they were few and far between, and the witnesses were discredited due to their histories of drunk and disorderlies. A few women reported having been lured from their bedrooms by a handsome man with brightly glowing, teal eyes and pointy incisors. They claimed to have been bitten on the neck as he drew their blood. They, too, were written off—female hysterics due to their monthlies, the puncture wounds in their necks said to have been self-inflicted. These reports coincided with the rise in popularity of Bram Stoker's *Dracula*, which led the authorities to speculate that, in their hysteria, the women had emulated iconic scenes in the book in which Dracula similarly woos Lucy and Mina. Stories such as these were no doubt used to bolster the opinion women weren't stable enough to vote, own land, or make decisions of import.

The last historical articles dated to the 1950s, when blood banks had, no doubt, become widespread and there was no longer the need for live donors, with or without consent. Modern articles picked up a few months ago coincided with reports of cougar-sightings in and around the Greater Toronto Area. In each case, the neck had been the target, and the resulting attack so damaging, I doubted they'd have found evidence of puncture wounds as the "hysterical" historical women averred.

There was a knock at my door, almost timid. I panicked at first, worried someone was in my apartment, but then I remembered bolting and chaining the front door before I'd settled in. What might be called paranoid at first glance seemed perfectly logical behaviour, given the fact the only "person" that could have possibly been there with me was my tulpa, Prudence. The last time I'd sat inside a salt circle, I'd "heard" her voice in my head. This time, either Pru was conspicuously silent—an anomaly, given how vocal and forthcoming she'd been of late—or the double lines of salt acted as force fields not only of body, but of mind.

I organized the pictures from the safety deposit according to date, based on my knowledge—such as it was—of fashion across the decades. The oldest image appeared to be the one I'd scrutinized at the bank, the one of Piers, Seph, and myself in Victorian garb. Most of the photos depicted the three of us in roughly the same pose, wearing costumes from different eras: at Kew Beach in what had passed for swimsuits at the turn of the twentieth century; Flappers in long fringes on a night on the town in the twenties; Piers in a soldier's uniform and Seph and I in pencil-skirts in the forties; and so on. Like the articles, the pictures tapered off sometime in the nineties, no doubt due to the proliferation of digital photography and the downturn in needing photographic prints to preserve moments in posterity.

Another knock at my door. This time it sounded more like fist-pounding; Pru was getting impatient.

I had a choice to make, and I needed to make it without Pru. Possession was nine-tenths of the law. Since I was currently inhabiting my body, it was, therefore, *my* decision to make.

Another bang at the door—loud enough, it seemed, to shake the foundations—underscored the fact that Pru was acting like a disgruntled landlord trying to out a squatter.

There was another bang, even louder, if that was possible, and I wished I'd thought to bring a set of noise-cancelling headphones with me.

I ticked off the facts:

- I was once Prudence, and she was once me;
- she and Piers had fallen in love;
- rather than grow old and be without him, she'd convinced Piers to change her into a blood-sucking, throat-tearing monster;
- rather than grow old and be without me, Seph had convinced Piers to do the same to her;
- the three of us had been together for more than a hundred years;
- I'd spent time as a creature of the night, feasting on people to survive;
- at some point, I'd switched to donated blood;
- like an alcoholic, I found it hard to switch from beer on tap to ginger ale, fell off the wagon, and had begun to feed again;
- full of self-loathing at what I'd become, I approached Percival to evict Pru with ancient magicks;
- afraid he wasn't skilled enough to pull the spell off, Percival had handed it's casting to someone who turned out to be even less competent than he;

- I was left in a pickle, trying to decide between the devil I knew (living with an uncontrollable tulpa), and the devil I didn't (integration with Pru).

Having summed my situation up, I was really no closer to solving my dilemma than I had been before.

My bedroom door burst open with the sound of cannon fire. I turned to see Pru hovering in the hall. The blast—strong enough to practically tear the door from its hinges—had blown some of the salt away, thinning the line but leaving enough of it behind for my force field to hold.

I still couldn't hear what she had to say, but I could feel her anger at being cowed to silence where my decision was concerned.

It was enough to sway my verdict.

She was dispossessed. She was angry. She was dangerous. She was strong, and her strength only seemed to be growing.

We'd been asking the wrong question all along. Rather than search for a way to merge us back into one, we needed to look for a way to cut the ties that bind, exorcising her from my life, one and for all.

Percival was wiping the bar down when I arrived at Stoker's. He was wearing a light blue and aqua plaid shirt which brought out the blue in his eyes. When he saw me approach, he looked up, smiled, and nodded. "What can I get for you, sweetheart?"

"Something tall, blond, and smarmy…oh, wait…"

Percival chuckled. "The usual?"

I sighed. "I guess." The establishment functioned as a restaurant during the day, but it was empty. Probably the lull between lunch and the demand for blood-laced cocktails served by the light of the moon. A brutal murder happening on the premises didn't help. "I find it unsettling that you know my preferences better than I do."

"Well," he said, putting a glass of pee-coloured liquid with a blob of something sanguine hovering under the ice in front of me, "it shouldn't…given the circumstances.

"One blood bag cocktail." I glanced up from the tall glass in front of me. "Relax," he said, detecting my alarm. "It's a double-virgin: orange juice and club soda with raspberry puree." He moved his hand in a swiping motion. "No alcohol, no blood. It works best if you stir before drinking." He plunked a plastic stir stick into the glass.

"We need to talk," I said, stirring.

Percival leaned on the bar with his elbows and rested his chin in his hands. "So…talk."

I looked around to make sure no one was within earshot. "Curatorial stuff," I whispered.

"Oh," he said, standing. "Piers is unavailable until—"

"I don't need Piers; I need you."

"Oh, baby," he said, his lips curling into a huge, self-important grin.

"Cut it out, Percival. You know what I mean."

"Boy, do I ever."

"You know what?" I said, standing. "Just forget it. I'll figure it out on my own."

Percival reached over the bar to grab my wrist. "What you're asking is suicide—"

"I don't care."

"For me. It's suicide for *me*. If Piers finds out—"

I tried to pull my hand from his grasp, but he held fast. When I looked up at him with a questioning glance, he let go. "He won't find out. Whatever you do…whatever *we* do, I'll take all the blame."

He seemed to consider my proposal for a moment before saying, "What do you need?"

"Not here," I told him.

"The place has been warded against spirits and other supernatural beings."

"But Piers—"

"Piers is the exception. He has a spell-bag I made for him that allows him to enter."

"So Prudence—"

"Technically, tulpas aren't supernatural beings, but I think Prudence may be the exception to the rule."

"We'll need salt."

"The wards should pre-empt the need for salt."

"Do you have any?"

"There's a whole store of it inside," he said, turning the key in the lock.

"When I needed some alone time, I put a line of salt across the doors and windows and made another circle around myself. The double-salt line was like a cone of silence, keeping Pru at bay."

He closed the door behind us and was reaching for the light switch while I spoke, but now he turned and said, "Wait…you saw Pru again?"

"I summoned her," I said quietly and advanced further into the library.

"Why would you go and do something stupid like that?"

"Salt?" I asked. Percival pointed down a hallway and took the lead.

"Not stupid at all. I learned quite a bit about myself, Piers, *and* Seph."

"Ah…the love triangle to end all love triangles."

"What do you know about it?"

Percival opened a closet door, turned the light on inside, handed me a kilogram-sized bag of salt, took one for himself, and motioned me back out the door. "Most guys like Piers drink whole blood as food. Plasma alone, however—the liquid the red blood cells are stored in—that works more like an

150

intoxicant. Let's just say Piers has been known to…imbibe every once in a while, and when he does, he grows quite chatty."

I chuckled. "That sounds like something I'd pay to see."

"Suffice it to say, you can chalk your little love triangle up as another unsettling aspect of your life."

We went back to the main part of the library, drew a salt line across the only entrance and a thicker line to delineate a large circle around one of the work tables. When we were done, we left the salt bags outside of the circle, and each of us took a seat inside the circle at the table.

"What can I do you for?" Percival asked, leaning back in his chair. He put his feet up on the table and crossed his legs at the ankles.

"Up until now," I started, leaning toward his side of the table, "we've been operating under the premise that the only way to get rid of Prudence is to put the two of us back together. What if there's a way to get rid of her totally? Like…stay me but without her?"

Percival brought his feet down onto the floor with a stomp and leaned forward in his chair. "That book—*Tulpamancy for Dummies*? It says the only way to get rid of a tulpa is through visualization—"

"How do I do that?" I asked excitedly, thinking I could finally see the light at the end of the tunnel.

"You visualize a door, imagine your tulpa walking through it, and shut the door behind it—"

I shook my head. "Pru and I tried that after I summoned her, but it didn't work."

"That makes sense. You don't have a tulpa, Addison. That was just the closest analogy I could think of to describe it. What you have isn't like an infestation—you can't exterminate it.

"Prudence is you, without her—"

"What's the worst that could happen?"

"Let me rephrase that: without *you*, Prudence is beyond dangerous.

"You asked me, so I'm going to be straight with you: Prudence is a killer. She always has been, ever since she was made. The worst that could happen is that you live in the wake of her blood storm. Eventually, one of those detectives is going to realize you're the common thread between all of her victims. They'll blame you, and you'll go down in history as a spree killer—"

"Spree killer?"

"Someone who kills in bursts instead of over a long period of time.

"They'll catch you and lock you away for a very long time. And still, the murders will continue. Imagine the feast Prudence will have in a place like prison—she'll make it her own, personal slaughterhouse."

"So, what do I do?"

"Help me research for a way to bind the two of you back together."

I leaned back in my chair, somehow keeping my tears of frustration at bay. "The only way out of this is for me to become the killer?"

Percival reached across the table and motioned for me to take his hand.

"Aren't you worried about Piers?" I asked, entwining my fingers with his.

"Piers isn't here to comfort you now."

I picked my hand up off the table without letting go of his. "Is that what you call this?"

"I'd have to be stupid fifty ways to Sunday to make a pass at you, especially now.

"What I was going to say was that I don't see another way to stop the killing."

"What makes you think I'll be able to stop her? What if her need to feed is stronger than my ability to control it?"

"You've been able to control it for as long as you've been on the bag—"

"Until I couldn't anymore...I mean, until *she* couldn't anymore."

"The way I see it, you're like any other addict—"

"Addicted to blood directly from the jugular?"

He nodded. "So, you fell off the wagon. Fine. It's not like you're the only one. You can pick yourself up, dust yourself off, and redouble your efforts. You may have lost your hundred-year chip, but you can start again, twenty-four hours at a time."

I let go of his hand and leaned back in my chair again. "I'd be lying if I said I wasn't scared."

To say I was scared was an understatement. If Prudence was me, as Percival had said, what might happen once we joined? He'd also said Prudence needed me, but that didn't mean she'd let me have control. Plenty of people had nasty co-dependent relationships—I wondered how many of them had one with another facet of themselves.

"So would I." I must've looked at Percival weirdly, because he said, "Be lying if I said I wasn't scared."

"Where do we start?"

"I know you said you didn't need Piers, but we have to read him in on this."

"Why are you so scared of him?"

He looked at me as if I'd begun to speak in tongues. "You saw what Prudence can do, and that's not even with real teeth."

I didn't get what he was trying to say at first—didn't everyone have teeth that were real?

Percival let out a breath through an open-mouthed grin. "He hasn't shown you his teeth yet, has he?"

"I've seen Piers' teeth," I said, defensively. His teeth were pearly white and straight as a bunch of teeny-tiny peppermint Chicklets.

"You've seen his teeth, but have you seen his *teeth*?"

I shook my head.

"Piers baring his teeth, eyes a-glowing, is a sight you'd wished you'd never seen. I've...donated blood to him every once in a while. I know the kind of damage he's capable of inflicting when he sees red."

"Fine. Piers is in. What about Seph?"

"Piers and Seph don't get along."

"But Seph and *I* do."

Percival winked and plastered a dirty smile on his lips. "Don't I know it."

"Mind out of the gutter, *Percy*."

He shook his head and looked at his watch. "Piers should be awake in a couple of hours. We can call him after official sundown time and read him in then."

Pervical spent the rest of the day researching in his archives. I sat in Stoker's nurturing blood bag cocktails. I was on my fourth when Piers arrived just after sundown. He sat on the stool next to me at the bar and said, "Am I too late?" nodding at the drink in my hand.

"It's a double-virgin," I told him. He looked confused, so I added, "No blood, no liquor."

"Ah," he said, nodding. He got the bartender's attention from the other end of the bar and pointed at my drink.

"Another double-virgin?" he asked.

Piers smiled and said, "Ah, no…I'd like an actual blood bag…er…the cocktail, not the…you know."

Percival seemed to materialize from somewhere behind the bar to say, "No imbibing for you tonight, mister." Piers knit his eyebrows together and frowned. "Sir," Percival added. He shooed the bartender away and said, "We have work to do, and everyone needs to be sober to do it."

"Everyone?" Piers asked.

"Hello, Piers, darling," a female voice—which I immediately recognized as Seph's—intoned from behind us. My heart skipped a beat or two. She came up to me, put her arms around my midsection from behind, and kissed me on the cheek. "Addie, love." I didn't know what game she was playing or whether she was playing it with Piers or me. Given the fact he was sitting right next to me, sneering as he took everything in, given the way my body had reacted to her touch, I'd say it was probably with both of us.

"Hail, hail, the gang's all here," Piers muttered. He took a swig of his double-virgin and grimaced. "Percival, brother," he locked his verdant greens onto Percival's, his jaw clenched, "I need a drink."

I put my hand on Piers' which was resting on the bar and shook my head.

"Fine," he said. "Nevermind." To Percival, he said, "I release you."

Percival responded, "Have I ever told you how much I dislike it when you do that?"

Piers scowled and mumbled something unintelligible.

"Let's get this shit show on the road, shall we?" Percival continued without missing a beat. He tossed a small, burlap, spell-bag at Seph. "You'll need this," he told her.

Back in Pervical's library, Seph was having an epiphany, much the same as mine the first time Piers and Percival had introduced me to their set-up beneath the bar. "And this has been here the whole time Stoker's has?" she asked.

"It's actually been here longer," Percival said.

"Why haven't I heard of you guys before?"

"We're a secret society. We're good at keeping secrets."

"Well, *yeah*." Seph leaned over the railing to catch a glimpse of what lay beyond. "So were the Knights Templar and the Free Masons—"

"Extinct and not so secret anymore."

Piers and I sat at the table, our feet crunching on the remnants of the salt circle Percival and I had drawn earlier in the day. "You nervous?" he asked.

"A little," I said.

"This could be a good thing, you know."

I nodded. He took my hand and squeezed. "Whatever happens, I'm with you...all the way."

"No shit!" Seph said in response to something Percival had told her. "What exactly does that mean...legacy?"

"It means I've inherited my title as curator, along with the building and its collection."

"Why a bar?" She had moved on from the railing and was checking out the ancient books and artifacts on the shelves nearby. "Wouldn't a book or occult store be more apropos?"

"Turning it into an after-hours bar gives me the opportunity to study the indigenous supernatural population in their natural habitat, so to speak."

"Can we get on with it," Piers said loudly, "before this member of the indigenous supernatural population wants to feed in his natural habitat?"

"Yes," Percival said, nervously, "of course." I got the feeling he realized Piers couldn't feed off Seph, and he wouldn't feed off me, which meant *he* would be the obvious take-out if Piers decided to go on a food run.

Percival pulled a wooden library cart up, removed a laptop from it, and opened it. While he waited for it to resume, he opened a book, a large, old volume that smelled of dampness and decay. "So far, we've been calling Pru a tulpa, but basic metaphysics—abstract concepts such as time, seeing, knowing, being, et cetera—pretty much negates the idea of a tulpa ever manifesting as a physical being. Ancient Tibetan manuscripts seem to confirm this—"

"You read ancient Tibetan?" I asked.

"Well, I'm not fluent, but...yes. I know quite a few ancient and/or dead languages. Have to in my line of work.

"Early on, Piers suspected Pru might be a spectre. The closest analogy I could find to that theory is a malevolent spirit, like a poltergeist, one who can cause physical disturbances, but Pru seems to be so much more than that."

"Speaking of Pru..." I said.

"She can't come in as long as the wards hold."

"Shouldn't she be in on the conversation?" Seph asked. "I mean, this concerns her, too, doesn't it?"

"It does," Percival confirmed, "but whatever solution we come up with should primarily concern Addison's well-being, and Pru might have other ideas."

Seph continued, "I just think—"

"Addison's still alive, Seph," Piers said. "We need to do what we can to keep it that way."

"How do I know you're not just interested in being with a warm body and keeping control of a potential food source?"

Piers' eyes flashed metallic green, and I wondered if I'd finally get to see those teeth Percival had spoken of.

"We all know Pru's dangerous on her own, and we all have Addison's best interests at heart. Our goal is to successfully unite the two as soon as possible. We also know how much the two of you care about our girl, here," Percival said. I felt myself blush. "The two of you getting into a pissing contest isn't going to help any, so what say we put our differences aside and get on with the issue at hand?"

Piers nodded at Percival. Seph also nodded.

"Good," Percival said. "We know Pru's not a poltergeist, nor is she an intelligent, malevolent spirit." He turned to his laptop. "If we look to the Dark Web, we see a number of incantations designed to Jekyll and Hyde people, but there's no mention of the Jekyll hanging around and killing people, nor is there any mention of how to put the two parts together once rend asunder."

"Bottom-line it for us already," Piers told him.

"The barista cast some sort of home-brewed spell, creating something one of a kind. I've sent feelers out in some of the chat rooms on the Dark Web, but since no one's ever seen this before, no one knows how to cure it."

"Great," I said.

"Hope's not lost," Percival said.

"Maybe next time you want to lead with that?" I asked.

"Still waiting for the bottom line," Piers said, sounding bored.

"I have the Jekyll and Hyde spell." He switched to the book he'd pulled from the dolly and opened it to a bookmarked page. "If we think of the ingredients in the original spell as the Yin, all we have to do is find each of their Yangs, say the incantation in reverse, and we should be able to reverse the spell."

"Do you know the Yang for the ingredients?" Seph asked.

"I do."

"Well, then, what are we waiting for?" Piers said.

"There's only one problem: the original recipe calls for a drop of blood—"

"No problem there," I said. "I have plenty of that."

"It has to be a drop of blood from *before* the barista's spell."

"How do you figure that?" Piers asked. I couldn't tell if he was frustrated or angry.

"Blood is the catalyst for the spell. In the original spell, the blood works to focus it. It takes the united blood and separates it into two halves, but you're already separated. You need your blood from before the barista's spell in order to join your two halves."

"Any idea how we can get that?" I asked the group. Both Piers and Seph shook their heads.

"Wait," Piers said after a beat, "the amulet you are wearing."

I held the pendant in my hand and lifted the chain from around my neck. "What about it?" I asked, putting it on the table in front of me.

"I purchased it for her before I turned her. She was worried about forgetting her humanity after the change, so we had a drop of her blood sealed up in it as a reminder of what she was before.

"Will that work?" Piers asked.

"It might." Percival reached across the table to take it.

"Will it be enough?" I asked.

He held the amulet up to the light, turning it first to the left, then to the right, as if trying to analyze its contents. Percival sighed. "It'll have to be."

"Wait a minute," Seph said. "If the blood is from *before* Pru turned, how do we know she'll still be in there after the ritual?"

"We don't," I said. I pushed my chair out from the table, stood behind Seph, and put my arms around her shoulders.

Piers grumbled.

"I'm sorry, Seph, but this is the only way. We can't let her go on killing everyone I come into contact with, or I'll wind up spending the rest of my life behind bars. At least this way, you'll still have some of her around."

She took hold of my hand and squeezed; I practically felt the anger radiating from Piers in a wave of heat.

"So, it is settled," Piers said.

Percival handed each of us a list. "If we divide and conquer to find the ingredients, the search will go quicker."

I checked out my portion of the ingredients, which read like a grocery list. "Anise?" I asked.

"That's a tweak of my own. Anise is known to help purify one's soul. We don't want you continuing Pru's bloodfest, now, do we?"

"How do you know your tweak, as you call it, will not affect the outcome of the ritual?" Piers asked.

"I'm flying blind as it is. We don't know there even *will* be an outcome to the ritual."

"Mint?" I said.

"To make the spell work faster. Be sure to get fresh and organic—I doubt dried will work in this scenario."

"Seriously…bat guano?" Seph said. "What's the Yin to that?"

"Slow flying insects," Percival answered. When no one responded, he added, "Bat food."

The three of us made a variety of sounds, indicating we'd made the connection.

"Twenty-four hours," Percival warned.

"Uh…problem," I said. "Prudence can read my thoughts. I don't know if she could before, but after I summoned her—"

"You summoned her?" Piers said, jumping to a standing position. "Why would you do that?"

"I needed information about my past, and you weren't exactly forthcoming," I said.

He came over and hugged me. "That was dangerous and foolish."

"It's not like she could eat me, or she'd have nowhere to go.

"We tried visualization to unite us, and it didn't work. I figured it was worth a shot."

"Who told you to try visualization?" Piers asked.

"Percival mentioned it, but I'd already heard it from Dr. Putnum."

"Who?"

"Dr. Putnum. The psychiatrist they assigned me right after I lost my memory."

"She's...human...right?"

It finally dawned on me why Piers seemed so alarmed. Shortly after I'd visited the Pumpkin Spice, Pru had killed the barista; I went to Stoker's for a drink, and she'd eaten the bartender; Piers' driver took me home, and she went to town on him, as well. "I need to call her," I said. I took my phone from my purse, found Dr. Putnum's name in my contact list, and pressed the call button to dial. It rang about five times before the voicemail picked up.

Five rings didn't seem like enough time to pick up a phone. Ten rings would be better. I tried again. Five more rings and voice mail kicked in. I looked up at Piers, feeling tears well in my eyes, and shook my head. "Can you take me to Dr. Putnum's office?" I asked.

Piers put his phone to his ear and said, "Already calling for a driver."

We held no high hopes Dr. Putnum would still be in her office, but it was the last place I'd seen her alive. Her office was on the fifth floor—Psychiatric Services. It was locked, which was no big surprise, but it also wasn't a guarantee of her safety.

Percival reached into his pocket and brought out a small, leather case and held it up between us, his lips curled into a greasy smile. Piers nodded, and Percival set about opening the case, removing some tools, and picking the lock.

"What if there's an alarm?" I asked.

Percival looked up at me, challenging. "We run."

There was no alarm.

"Dr. Putnum?" I called once inside, but there was no answer.

Percival picked the lock to her interview room, but she wasn't there, either. Also absent was any evidence blood had been spilled. I think we breathed a collective sigh of relief.

"Now what?" I asked.

"She probably wasn't offed elsewhere in the hospital, or she most likely would have been found by now," Percival said.

"How about some compassion?" Piers said.

Percival shrugged.

"We need to go to her home," I said.

"Where does she live?" Seph asked.

I shrugged my shoulders. "Her first initial's N. It says so on her business card."

"And on the door," Seph said.

Piers had his phone out. "There are too many N. Putnums in the Greater Toronto Area."

"What about Nancy?" Seph said.

"Nellie?" I asked.

"Ned?" Percival said.

Piers dropped the hand holding his phone to his side and gave Percival the kill-eye.

"Sorry, sir," he said, deferential.

"What about a reverse look-up of her cell number?" I asked.

"Doesn't work the same as with landlines," Percival said.

"But if she's posted it anywhere online…" Piers resumed his Internet search. "Bingo!" he said a moment later. "Nora Putnum. And if I search 'Nora Putnum address' I get…Got it! Let's go!"

Dr. Putnum's house—a huge residence circa 4,000 square feet as a conservative estimate—was surprisingly quiet when we arrived. We had Piers' driver drop us off a few doors away, and the four of us advanced up her driveway under the cover of night.

I knocked on the door, but there was no response. We waited a few moments before I knocked again, only this time, rather than being greeted with silence, a scream came from inside the house.

"Dr. Putnum?" I called, knocking on the door in rapid succession. "Let us in." When it was clear she wasn't about to do that, Piers spread his arms wide and took a few steps back, forcing us to do the same. He stomped his foot against the door, and it exploded into tiny splinters.

"Help!" we heard Dr. Putnum scream, no doubt having heard us, thinking she was about to be saved.

Piers hesitated before stepping over the threshold.

"Don't you have to be invited in?" Percival asked.

"She called for help," I said. "I'd say that's about as close to an invitation as you're going to get."

We advanced to the back of the house where we found the kitchen, awash in blood spatter. My first step into the room hit a puddle of blood, and I slipped. I would have fallen had Seph not caught me.

She flashed me a smile. "I've got your back."

"Literally." I returned the grin.

We walked a bit further into the kitchen. "Prudence?" I asked.

Piers turned the corner around the kitchen counter. "Oh," he said.

"What?" I asked.

"Stay there." He'd tried to save me from the sight, but it was too late. Dr. Putnum's husband was on the floor in a rapidly spreading pool of blood, his throat ripped out, a big hole in his chest where his heart should've been.

Black spots clouded my vision.

"She's escalating," Percival observed.

Bitter gall rose at the back of my throat. The room started to spin. My stomach churned—it was all I could do to keep everything together.

"Not here," Percival said. "You can't chance leaving your DNA behind."

I ran to find a washroom, opening doors at random, noting to remember to wipe down each and every door handle and clean up each and every bloody footprint I left behind me. When, at last, I found the washroom, I hunched over the toilet and heaved.

I was responsible for his death. It was *my* fault. All of it.

I retched into the toilet, hoping to expel whatever it was tethering me to the monster I'd unleashed.

Pru was my fault. I'd been unhappy. I'd gone to an amateur. I'd allowed her to perform home-grown, faulty magick on me.

Dr. Putnum screamed again, snapping me out of my funk. I heard everyone rush toward the sound. I flushed the toilet and returned to the kitchen, trying to remember how I'd gotten Pru to materialize back at my condo. If I could just divert her attention long enough for Piers *et al.* to get Dr. Putnum out of the house, I might be able to reason with her and let her in on our plan. "I summon you, Prudence," I said.

No, that wasn't quite right.

"Prudence?" I said, my voice catching in my throat. "Prudence!" I called a bit louder, but that still wasn't quite right.

Then it dawned on me: "I call on you, Prudence!" I shouted, trying to sound as strong as I could. "Here and now, Prudence—I call on you."

A rush of frigid air descended upon me, followed by Prudence in a grey mist.

I am hungry, she said. *Do you not know it is not wise to disturb...whatever it is I am when I am eating?*

"I must've missed that lesson in my tulpamancy class."

To retain your sense of humour in the face of death...you and I are a lot more alike than you would care to admit. She swirled around me, changing shape as she did. Now she was an amorphous blob. Now she was a helix, twisting and turning, engulfing me in the eye of her storm.

"You can't kill Dr. Putnum," I told her. "I won't allow it."

She floated up toward the ceiling, looking every bit like a raincloud. *You shut me out earlier with your double-salt lines and your wards. You didn't want to talk to me then, what makes you think I want to talk to you now?*

"Is that what this is? A bid to regain my attention?"

It worked, did it not? She swooped toward the floor near Mr. Putnum's body as if admiring her handiwork.

Guilt seeped back into my consciousness. All of this—another murder, terrorizing someone who had tried to help—because she'd felt slighted? My stomach did a flip-flop, but this wasn't the time to back down.

A great galumphing of footsteps pounded down the main stairway.

No! Pru shouted. She rushed toward the front door, which had slammed shut only seconds before she reached it, and she shrieked in anger and frustration. When she returned to the kitchen, she said, *What makes you think I will not go after them?*

"The police are no doubt on their way. We need to take care of our business here and go."

The front door opened again, and I heard Pervical shout, "Addison?"

I am hungry, Pru said, and she floated in Percival's direction.

"You can't have Percival," I told her, racking my brain for the phrase Piers had used the first time we'd met, just before he'd punched Percival in the nose. "He is mine."

He is yours? How does Piers feel about that?

"It's not what you think," I said.

"Uh…Addison? Who are you talking to?"

"Prudence," I told him.

"She's here?"

"You can't see her?"

I choose to sneak up on my prey. It makes the hunt more interesting.

"Show yourself," I commanded.

I assumed she complied because Percival asked, "That mist…that's her?"

"Can he hear you?" I asked Pru.

No.

I shook my head to indicate to Percival she'd answered in the negative. "You can't eat Percival. He's our last hope at fixing this," I told her.

Do you agree to join with me?"

"Provided you follow through with what you promised: that you'll curb your appetite—no more killing."

Percival elbowed me. "What's she saying?"

I find him annoying. I might just go ahead and kill him after he has outlived his usefulness.

I was silent for a moment, wondering what I might say in answer to Percival's question.

Kidding, Pru said. *I am kidding. I promise not to kill the annoying human, even when I no longer consider him useful.*

"What's she saying?" Percival asked again.

"She agrees," I told him.

Percival placed the ingredients we'd collected into a cast iron pot. We gathered around the table, spreading the remnants of our salt circle everywhere, grinding it into the soles of our shoes and the spaces between the linoleum tiles—it would be a bitch to clean.

"Amulet," Percival said, holding out his hand.

It was a pretty necklace, and I was sorry to see it go, but what weighed more heavily on my mind was how I'd come out on the other side of the ritual that was about to happen. If I thought Pru had been scary before, she'd just proven she was downright terrifying.

Poor Dr. Putnum sat in a chair by the doorway, near catatonic. Though some would admonish her with a "Physician, heal thyself," I couldn't really blame her for being in shock. She had, after all, just witnessed the brutal maiming of her husband and thought she would be the next victim of an invisible, supernatural stalker.

"She is going to be okay," Piers told me, having noticed I was staring at her.

"I wouldn't be so sure," I told him. Dr. Putnum didn't deserve this. She'd done nothing but try to help me, help Pru, and her life had been turned upside down in a widow-making event by way of thanks.

Piers affected a grin that made me uncomfortable. "Nothing that a few years of therapy would not cure," he said with a wink.

I rolled my eyes and turned my attention back to Percival, who had placed the amulet in the pot. "There's one more thing we need," he said. He held out a pair of handcuffs.

"The woman couldn't hurt a fly," I said, thinking they were for Dr. Putnum. "I don't think we need those."

"They're...not for the doctor," Percival explained.

"Oh," I said once realization had dawned. "Why?"

"They're not for you, either," Percival said.

"They're for Pru," Seph concluded.

Percival nodded. "We can't be sure what will happen once she bonds with you. We need to consider every contingency."

Piers pulled a chair out from under the table and positioned it in the middle of the room. I nodded and sat. Percival handed two pairs of handcuffs to Piers and the men set to cuffing my wrists and ankles to the chair.

"These are iron," Percival said.

"I thought iron was supposed to *repel* evil spirits," Seph said. "Won't that prevent Pru from joining with her?"

"Ordinarily, yes," Percival said, "but I've warded them in such as way as to let the supernatural in, but not out."

Piers looked up at me as he fastened the last handcuff, one link around the chair leg, the other around my ankle. "Too tight?" he asked.

I shook my head. "I'm good." I wasn't. Good, I mean. I was scared in ways that couldn't be measured. We were about to summon an evil spirit to inhabit my body, and I'd been rendered powerless to help myself in the event something went wrong. I remembered what Pru had said to me back in Dr. Putnum's kitchen, that she and I were a lot more alike than I cared to admit, and I shuddered.

"What about Dr. Putnum," I asked. "Isn't she at risk, sitting there near comatose like that?"

Everyone turned to look at the woman.

"She has a point," Seph said.

"Take her to my bedroom," Percival said.

"This place has bedrooms?" she asked.

"One. I converted a boardroom into a bedroom."

"You live here?"

Percival shrugged. "Beats paying rent."

"Can we trade real estate secrets later, please?" I asked.

"Right," Percival said. "Down that hall." He pointed. "Third door on your left."

The three of them looked at each other as if mentally debating who should be the one to take her. Finally, Piers turned to Seph and said her name as if pleading. "Please," he added. "We will wait for your return."

It seemed to take forever for Seph to usher the doctor to Percival's converted bedroom. Once she'd returned, Percival said, "Let's fuse this sucker!" He nodded to Piers who picked up a box cutter, went over to the door, and scratched at one of the symbols that had been painted around the jamb; Percival's "wards", I assumed.

No sooner had he returned to the group than Pru materialized from under the door in a grey cloud. She swooped in and circled around me before coalescing and hovering above my head like my own personal raincloud.

I do not approve, she told me. *If the human is successful in this endeavour, I will be confined to the chair.*

"You won't be able to hurt anyone," I told her.

"What did she say?" Piers asked.

As if she'd just noticed he was in the room, Pru floated over to Piers and formed a corkscrew around him. Piers seemed stunned, to say the least. His expression told me he was calculating if Pru would be able to hurt him in her current form.

Something was off. If Piers had loved Prudence so much as to convince me to go ahead with the possession rather than figure out a way to eradicate her from our lives, why did he seem so scared?

Pru returned to her holding pattern above my head. *I will take him and make him beg for more*, she said, dripping with avarice. She floated over to Seph and formed a helix around her. *And then I will take her and eat her pretty little girlfriend for supper.*

"Uh...guys?" I said, horrified at what I'd just heard. "Are you sure this is a good idea?"

"It's a little late for that sentiment, isn't it?" Percival said.

"Um...no. No, it's not. Pru's dangerous. If you could only hear what she's saying—"

Yes, my dear, Addison, tell them what I am saying.

"You're cuffed," Percival said. "Prudence will be cuffed. You'll be fine."

"I'm not the one I'm worried about," I told them. "Back at Dr. Putnum's place, she threatened your life, Percival. She said she'd kill you when you were no longer of use to her."

173

"So?"

"She won't need you once the ritual's done."

"I'm touched that you're so concerned about me, but I'll be fine—"

"No…no you won't. And neither will Seph's girlfriend.

"We need to abort," I told them. "Abort and go back to finding a way to kill her instead."

You cannot kill me, Pru hissed, *not without you dying, as well.*

"I'm willing to take that risk," I shouted. The room quieted. "She's taunting me," I told them. "She thinks if she appeals to my sense of self-preservation I'll want to go ahead with this, but I don't care about that anymore."

Piers dropped to a knee beside me and took my hand in his. "Addison," he said quietly, "*I* care. I love *you*, with or without Pru inside."

Of all the knavish, shifty—

"You were the one I fell for. Pru was who you became once you'd been turned."

—unprincipled, treacherous—

"She's mad," I told him.

Pru broke off her litany of name-calling.

"We need to go ahead with this," I told him, fully planning to end both of our lives if the merge was successful. "There can be no more murders as a result of my initial stupidity. I won't allow any more blood to accumulate on my hands."

"I won't point out the irony behind that statement," Percival said.

Piers looked at him and growled. "Are you sure?" he asked me.

I nodded. "Once Pru's bound to me and in physical form, you need to kill her if she steps out of line."

I would like to see him try, Pru grumbled.

I squeezed his hand. "I give you permission to kill us if she steps out of line."

Piers nodded, stood, and turned to Percival. "Time to fuse this sucker!" he said.

Percival began a series of incantations in a language I couldn't identify. He lit a match and threw it on the pile of ingredients in the cauldron-like pot, waved his arms over the top of it, and repeated the incantation.

I began to feel nauseated and started to heave, a great series of exhalations from within, each of them threatening to tear my lungs from my body and take my throat with them. When, at last, I was able to breathe in a gulp of air, Pru's great, dark cloud came with it.

My body grew cold. The room was silent save the sound of a single, beating heart. It took me a moment to realize it wasn't mine. I took a deep breath, forcing my chest to expand. Along with the sensation of my lungs filling came the understanding that it was the first breath I had taken in a while.

Piers knelt beside me and took my hand. I turned to look at him and smiled. How I longed to feel his lips on mine again. "Addison?"

My smile turned to a grimace. "You wish," I berated. "*She* was the one you fell for?" I asked, putting all the venom I could behind the first word. "*I* was what she became? After I gave up everything I knew to be with you…you should be ashamed of yourself, Piers, darling."

"They were but parting words," he said with a self-deprecating chuckle. "She is nothing but a memory now."

"Speaking of memory—I remember. I remember it all, as Addison, as Pru, and as Addison once more.

"You made love to her—"

"I made love to *you*, to what you had become," he apologized. "We had no idea—"

"You had condemned me to the ether?"

"Something like that."

My stomach rumbled. "I am hungry," I said, but it was more than that, more than simple hunger. It was as if my entire body cried out for sustenance, from the ends of my length of hair to the tips of my toes.

"Here," Percival said. He tossed a blood bag—an actual blood bag, not that silly cocktail—at Piers who cracked it open and held it to my lips.

I took a few gulps, feeling it spread through my system, nourishing my soul. As incredible as it felt, there was something off about it, an aftertaste similar to that left behind by artificial sweeteners. "It tastes funny," I told Piers once he had pulled the bag away.

"They put additives in the blood to prevent it from coagulating," Piers explained. "You will get used to it."

"I will not," I said.

Piers gave me a stern look and said, "You had better. That was the deal, remember? A steady diet of bagged blood in exchange for reuniting with Addison."

"Stop referring to me in the third person," I told him. "I am as much Addison as I am Prudence. I remember it all: Pru's feeding and history and Addison's fear and remorse."

"Then do not test my limits, Pru. You also agreed to be put down if you could no longer control yourself."

"I am aware." I looked him in the eyes, noting how much weaker the pull of them felt than when I had been only Addison. "More blood, please," I said after a pause. Piers complied, holding the bag to my mouth until I had drained it. When he pulled the empty bag away, I said, "Why am I still chained?" I pull the ones at my wrists taut.

"You will remain chained until you are able to control yourself."

I tuned into the sound of the beating heart again, recognizing it as Percival's. I imagined how it would feel to sink my teeth into his jugular, to feel the blood spurt as his heart contracted again and again, pumping the ruby liquid into my mouth, and how much how much I would enjoy feeling the flow of blood slow to a trickle and then stop entirely.

Though I had to admit they had a point, I pulled at the chains again and said, "I can control myself."

"Pru?" Seph said. She walked around my chair and into my line of sight. "How are you?"

"Still hungry," I told her, "and room-temperature, processed blood isn't going to cut it."

"Heads up," Percival said, tossing another bag at Piers.

"It had better," Piers said, cracking the seal on the bag. "It is all you have."

I lowered my shoulders, forced a sigh, and nodded at Piers, who fed me once more.

This blew. And to make matters worse, I felt Addison inside me, protesting vociferously each and every time I mentioned being set free, and cheering each time Piers rejected my request. She was still in there, still in *me*. Whatever ritual Percival had set in motion had done nothing more than imprison me in the same body as my human self to nag at me for all eternity.

You promised, she kept repeating, *no more killing*.

She screamed when I shared my fantasy about sucking Percival dry.

"Very well," I told Piers when he'd pulled the newly-drained bag away.

"Better?" Seph asked.

"Better."

"You're not you when you're hungry," Percival said.

I recognized the tagline from the chocolate bar commercial. "Very funny. Why don't you come a little closer, and I will show you just how funny it is?" I said, flashing him my teeth.

Addison commanded my tongue for a moment to run it over my canines, and I felt her recoil in horror.

Though I could not see the sunset or the rise of the moon, I knew it was night time. My friends and captors had decided to take feeding shifts. Percival was upstairs, busying himself with the day-to-day machinations of the bar. I had no idea where Piers was. Seph was somewhere in the library, in awe at the sheer number of books and artifacts collected over the centuries by generations of curators.

Given the time, I was at my most alert. I could hear the thump-thump beat of the music melded with the dull lub-lub of hundreds of hearts racing as they danced overhead.

The sound of stocking feet padding on the linoleum floor of the archives grew louder, nearer, more insistent.

"What is going on here?" a female voice said. Though the last time I'd heard the voice was in the throes of a shrill scream, I recognized it as belonging to Dr. Putnum. "Why is my patient chained to the chair?" It took her a moment to realize where she was. "What am I doing here?" Another moment passed before it dawned on her. "The last thing I remember—"

"Help me, Dr. Putnum," I said.

"What happened, Addison?" She pulled at the chain around my left wrist. When she kneeled down, I heard her heartbeat, sounding every bit as if someone were standing behind me, beating the rhythm of her heart on a drum. Her hair was up, and I could see her jugular, pulsing to the beat.

Nooooo! Addison shouted.

"How can I help you?" Dr. Putnum asked.

"You can't," Seph said, apologetically. "The best thing you can do is to back away from her."

Dr. Putnum stood, but she did not back away. "Who are you?"

"A friend," Seph said.

"If you're truly a friend, you'd let her go."

"I can't do that," Seph said, advancing on us. Dr. Putnum retreated a step for each one Seph took.

"What *is* this place?" Dr. Putnum asked. "Why am I here?"

"You're here because we saved you from the thing that killed your husband," Seph said.

Dr. Putnum gasped.

I took exception to being called a thing, but if the shoe fit...

"I need to go," Dr. Putnum said. "Where are my shoes?"

"I can't let you go, Doctor. Not just yet."

"Why not?"

"Because I can't leave Pru alone."

"Pru?"

"You know her as Addison."

"Why can't you leave her alone?"

"She's dangerous?"

"Addison's not dangerous," Dr. Putnum said. "Certainly not while she's chained up like this."

180

Et tu, Dr. Putnum?

That took a nasty turn quite quickly.

First, she was insisting I be let go, incensed at seeing one of her patients held captive, then she was willing to let it go so long as Seph was willing to take her back to the surface. It was an example of the human imperative for self-preservation at its best.

"Addison's not dangerous," Seph confirmed, "but Pru is. And right now, Prudence and Addison are one and the same."

"So, just let *me* go. I promise I won't tell anyone."

"I can't give up our location," Seph said. "You need to sit down until one of us can take you home."

They had planned to cover her face, take her home, look her in the eyes, and convince her she had slept through her husband's bludgeoning. Call it what you will—glamouring, compelling, or whatever—once turned, we had the power to make humans do whatever we wanted. All we had to do is to make eye contact, tell them what we wanted them to do, and they had no choice but to comply.

Seph quickly advanced on Dr. Putnum, put a hand on her shoulder, and walked her backward toward the nearest chair. She pushed her into it and then knelt before her, making eye contact. "You will sit here, quietly, until I am able to take you home."

Dr. Putnum nodded. "I will," she said absently.

Don't hurt her, Addison said.

"Oh, will you shut up already?" I said aloud.

"I beg your pardon?" Seph said, turning toward me.

"Addison is crying over her beloved saviour. She's afraid we are going to hurt her."

"What do you mean, Addison's crying?"

Whoops! I may have shown my hand all too soon.

Seph squatted in front of me. "Are you telling me there was no bond?"

"That's about the size of it."

"Poor Addison."

"Poor Addison? Poor me. I'm the one that has to listen to her whining twenty-four-seven."

I heard the door to the Library open behind me and footsteps. Based on the time between footfalls and the cadence of the heel-clicks, I knew it to be Piers.

Seph looked up at him over my shoulder. "We have a problem," she said.

It was Piers who suggested we go back to Dr. Putnum the day after we released her. Though my initial bloodlust had been sated, Piers did not want to take the chance with another driver, so he took us there himself.

Dr. Putnum's house was still strewn with yellow police tape. It was ironic that police services had chosen yellow tape to mark their crime scenes. Yellow was sunny and bright. Red was the colour of anger and blood, which made much more sense, given the circumstance of its use. Then again, yellow was also the colour of fear. Given the horrific nature of the crime I had perpetrated there, maybe yellow was a suitable colour after all.

Piers had decided it best for me to stay in the car—Dr. Putnum *was* human after all, and we didn't know how long I would be able to control my hunger. Though I had curbed the bloodlust, the hunger seemed to linger, always there at the back of my mind, reminding me to feed. Before he left to approach her door, he rolled the window down so I would be able to hear the conversation.

Dr. Putnum opened the door. "Go away." She tried to close the door, but Piers stuck a foot between it and the jamb. They had decided not to glamour her so she wouldn't forget the murder and mayhem that had ensued in her house, but nothing after Seph had spoken to her in the archives.

"I need your help."

"I don't know exactly what happened here, Mr.—"

"Westenra"

"Mr. Westenra, but I know it concerns you and my patient. Not to mention my husband is dead and my kitchen is drenched in his blood. I'd appreciate it if you went away."

"Addison needs your help."

She opened the door a little wider. "I would say both of you need help, and that's putting it mildly."

Dr. Putnum looked at me. I waved, but she dismissed it by looking away.

"You had her chained to a chair in a dungeon—"

"It was an archive—"

"Whatever it was, it was inappropriate to include me in it, to say the least."

"We saved your life," Piers told her.

Dr. Putnum glanced my way again. "I didn't tell the police anything. When they asked where I'd been, I told them I was in shock and wandering around the neighbourhood. I kept Addison out of it, because I recognize she's working through some serious issues. You, however, Mr. Westenra—I will have no such inclination to do the same for you if you don't get off of my property, never to return."

Though I felt pretty confident Dr. Putnum had no clue as to where we had kept her, she did know both of our names. The whole reason I'd agreed to go through the ritual was so I wouldn't leave any more breadcrumbs to allow the police to trace the murders back to me.

I gave Piers two short beeps on the car's horn to indicate we should go, but Piers was like a dog with a bone.

"Please, Dr. Putnum. We need your help," he pleaded. "*Addison* needs your help."

"Give me a minute," she said. Piers allowed her to close the door. When she returned, she had a card in one hand and her cell phone in the other. She handed Piers the card and said, "One of my colleagues. I'm sure he would be more than happy to take Addison on.

"This signifies the end of our business, Mr. Westenra. I have dialed 911. Whether or not you leave will determine whether or not I tell them I've pocket-dialed."

Piers nodded, thanked her, and returned to the car. Once inside, he handed me the card. "Her colleague," he said.

"Dr. Putnum aside, I think we need someone with more expertise than a simple shrink."

Piers started the car, and his phone rang. Because it had been connected to the dash via Bluetooth, the sound was broadcast through the stereo's speakers. The dashboard LCD display read "Percival". Piers pressed a button on his steering wheel to answer and said, "Yeah."

"We've got a problem here," Percival said. His voice was muffled, as if he were cupping a hand around the phone and his mouth.

"Not my circus," Piers said.

"But this does concern your monkeys," Percival replied. "Get over here, asap...*sir.*"

Percival was wiping down the bar when we arrived. The place had begun to fill with the after-dinner crowd. It would be a few hours before the establishment was crowded with the raunchier undead. DC Harker was sitting at a small, round table near the bar, nursing a Coke. My blood ran colder when I saw him...if that were at all possible. He stood when he saw us. "Ah, Miss Haney," he said, holding out a hand for me to shake. "Mr. Westenra." He shook Piers' hand as well.

"Detective...Harker, was it?" Piers said.

"You, sir, have a good memory."

Piers motioned for us to take a seat. Percival delivered each of us a drink before we had the chance to sit. I looked at my drink, frozen in a half-seated position, horrified that he might have served me a true blood bag cocktail. When I looked up at him, he said, "It's a double-virgin." My body relaxed into a full-seated position.

I took a sip of the cocktail and fought back a grimace. Though I knew the raspberry puree was made in-house from fresh, organic berries, it had a plastic aftertaste, nevertheless.

"Mr. Stoker and I had an interesting conversation in your absence," Harker told us.

"Who?" I asked, but I gleaned my answer when Percival pulled a seat up to join us.

"Any relation?"

"Distant," Percival answered, almost apologetically.

Harker snapped his fingers a few times in an attempt to garner our attention.

"Do not do that," Piers admonished.

"Percival?" Harker prompted.

"Harker's a hunter," Percival said.

Piers' eyes flashed emerald before he recoiled and shot from his seat, sending his chair halfway across the room.

"Way to rip the bandage off slowly," Harker said to Percival. To Piers, he said, "Relax. I'm not here to kill anyone…at least, not yet."

Percival got up to retrieve the chair, placed it behind Piers, and said, "Piers, please." When Piers didn't sit, Percival put a hand on his shoulder and seemed to guide him into the seat.

"Why are you here?" Piers asked once he had regained his composure.

"I'm sorry," I said, "a hunter?"

"Do you really need an explanation?" Percival asked. I had seen enough paranormal television to know what a hunter was, I just didn't think it was a thing. Then again, if tulpas and whatever I was were a thing…

"Harker's going to be setting up shop with me in the archives."

"Why?" Piers asked.

"It's the only way I could think to broker a deal to keep my patrons safe."

"Safe from what?" Piers asked.

"From me, of course," Harker said.

"I am sorry," I said. "You are a police officer, aren't you?"

"That was a cover."

"And the other guy…what was his name?"

"Reeves," Percival said.

"Another hunter. Joined me for backup."

"Why Percival?" Piers asked.

"Percy and I go way back," Harker said.

"We used to hunt, back before I inherited the archives."

"I thought your family were curators from way back," I said.

"They were, but I wasn't always interested in carrying on the family business."

My stomach grumbled. I looked at the double-virgin blood bag in front of me and considered taking another sip, but decided I needed something stronger. Though a drained double-Harker on ice sounded pretty good, I would settle for something alcoholic.

"His family wasn't happy about it, let me tell you," Harker said. "His dad said his ancestors were rolling over in their graves at the thought of it. He was always more into chronicling the efforts of others than joining the hunting parties himself."

"Wait," I said. "You're telling me *Dracula*—"

"Isn't a fiction," Percival said, "yes."

Harker let out a chuckle and settled back into his seat. "Don't tell me you're surprised. Given your situation, I'd have thought you'd already figured that out."

"What do *you* know of my situation?" I asked.

"More than you'd think, Addison, dear...or do you prefer Prudence now?"

It was my turn to recoil. I felt my teeth descend, and I lunged for him.

"Addison!" Piers shouted. I could practically feel every eye in the establishment turn to me, but I kept my sight focussed on the subtle throbbing at Harker's neck. "Prudence," Piers said, more of a warning, and I backed down.

It did not take long for Harker to regain his composure. He clapped his hands slowly, three times in succession. "What a performance," he said. "Encore." He looked at me, narrowing his eyes. "Please. Encore. Give me a reason to show you mine. Performance, I mean."

Percival waved at the bartender who came over. He whispered something to him, and he left. When the bartender returned, he was carrying a tray with four shot glasses on it. He put the tray down on the table and retreated back to the safety of the bar.

"A toast to our…unusual agreement," Percival said, helping himself to one of the glasses and holding it in the air.

"What agreement?" Piers asked.

Percival put the shot glass down in front of him. "Very well. Harker will be here as a deterrent—"

"He is your new bouncer," I offered.

"He'll be here as a deterrent to remind patrons of the…supernatural variety to remain in-line."

"And if they do not?" Piers asked.

Harker drew his pointer-finger across his neck.

"What is in the agreement for us?" Piers asked.

"You get to live," Harker said.

"You're my right-hand, Piers. Your kind will continue to come as long as you endorse this place."

Percival needed Harker as a deterrent. He needed Piers as an attraction. As far as I knew, I had no vested interest in the bar outside of Piers' hanging there. "Why do you need me?" I asked.

"To keep you in line," Harker said. "To keep all of you in line."

"I beg your pardon?" I said, even though I got it. All this time I had felt like a little girl lost, when I was really the loose cannon in the equation.

"Let's look at the facts, shall we? If you hadn't done your little sawing a girl in half trick gone wrong, I wouldn't be here in the first place. As for the rest of you: Stoker, here egged you on. When your witch wannabe messed it up, he covered it up rather than seek help. Piers and your little something-something on the side, Persephone, helped.

"Our agreement is that I promise not to wage war on your kind, and you promise to stay in line. Sounds like a win-win to me."

"And if we refuse?" Piers asked.

"Curators like Stoker, here, may be few and far between, but hunters are legion. If you refuse, I call my buddies, and we take you out."

"If hunters are so legion, why are you the first I have met in all of my years?" Piers said.

"Not unlike your kind, we have managed to operate under the radar for centuries. If you knew who we were, you'd wage war against us, and I'm not sure it's something we'd win without the element of surprise."

"Please, Piers," Percival said, "I need your help."

"Addison…Prudence…remains safe?" Piers said.

"As long as she keeps her hunger in check," Harker confirmed.

Piers lifted a shot glass. He looked at me and said, "I will protect you."

My heart, which had been quiet since the ritual, gave a rusty thunk. I also raised a glass. The other men followed suit.

I was born Prudence Hightower on Canadian soil in the year of our Lord 1855, the only daughter to British immigrants. I met my soul mate when I was nineteen and the love of my life when I was twenty-six.

When my love threatened to leave me, I begged him to make me more like him, but I have never been able to control the hunger as expertly as he.

I am an addict, addicted to blood, and I have fallen off the wagon a number of times over the years.

The modern era has made everything from travel to communication so much easier than when I was first turned. Everything, including feeding my hunger.

It is no longer necessary to kill to satiate my bloodlust, but blood bags taste processed. I much prefer my meat fresh, from farm to plate, so to speak. Along with this preference comes extreme guilt, shame, and regret, as is, I imagine, the case with all addicts. So when my love's sycophant suggested I see a witch to help me with my problems, I was happy to oblige.

The witch turned out to be a fraud, performing a home-grown type of magick, eliminating the bloodlust by clefting me in two—a human I christened Addison Haney and something darker. Addison was ruled by thought and feeling; Prudence, the darkness, ruled first and foremost by her hunger. The one thing I most needed purged, my guilt and self-loathing, remained.

Try as we might, there seemed no solution to my dilemma but to reunite myself with the dark half of my soul. I trusted the sycophant to do what was right, and I suppose it worked, but I am left with an insatiable craving for fresh blood that cannot be staved off with what comes in a bag.

I fear I may kill again.

Harker set up shop with Percival, clearing out an old safe full of ancient-looking artifacts to use as his office and residence. He liked the idea of being able to seal himself up in the room should things that go bump in the night find their way into the archives. Percival made him the bar's head of security, a position in name only, as it provided him with a reason to be there without arousing suspicion.

Seph opposed our agreement at first, but she eventually came around. She is happy going along with the deal, provided she is able to continue her research in order to find a solution to my problem. Her goal is to curb my cravings or do away with the darkness altogether. Percival has hired her to digitize his archives. It is more than one person could ever hope to accomplish given several lifetimes; who better than one of the undead to complete the task?

Piers continues to be the night manager at Stoker's. He has moved in with me so he can keep a closer eye on my behaviour and step in to save me, should the need arise. To lessen my bloodlust, he has turned his old place into a parlour of sorts, where he brings willing participants from which I feed. He pays them quite well, from a nest-egg he has amassed over the centuries. It took a while until I had trained myself to pull away before draining the donors dry, but I have since learned to tune into their circadian rhythm as I feed. I have gotten quite good at detecting minute changes in their heartbeats, breathing, and blood flow to know when I need to stop. At first, I fed on a donor a day, but Piers has gradually weaned me down to one a week. Like a drug addict who takes exceedingly smaller doses of methadone to lessen her dependence on a substance, Piers hopes to eventually rid me of my preference for fresh blood entirely. So far, it seems to be working.

Percival continues to run the bar, doing research on any new beings that wander in looking for a place that caters to things that go bump in the night, such as themselves. He and Harker catalogue everything they find in Seph's database.

Piers and Percival went in as partners to buy the Pumpkin Spice & Everything Nice. They hire the living to watch over the Everything Nice portion of the store, paying a commission to send anyone in need of a spell Percival's way. The hope is to avoid maimings that might be perpetrated by the next untrained barista while preventing any more people from falling prey to the darkness.

After the clean-up crew had set Dr. Putnum's house to right, she sold it. I showed up at her office one day, unannounced, begging her to see me. I told her my memory had returned and that I was grateful, but could not reconcile the two personalities in my brain. It was like there were two of us living in my head. No, I had not developed a case of dissociative identity—or multiple personalities—disorder, as Prudence seemed always in control. I was surprised when Dr. Putnum brought up the notion of a tulpa. I convinced her that I had heard her scream on the day her husband had died after she'd pocket-dialed me, and I'd brought my friends to investigate with me. And though it was weird the pocket-dial had not registered in her call history, she agreed to continue seeing me for as long as I needed.

Percival hired me as Stoker's *maître d'*. My spare time is spent in the Library archives, helping Seph look for a way to control my cravings without resorting to something as drastic as before. Though many humans frequent the bar, I am able to curb my bloodlust whilst sipping decidedly slutty blood bag cocktails.

The real challenge comes after hours, when I am in the archives in the presence of Percival and Harker, but Seph found a recipe for a potion that makes their blood taste like ass warmed over, which is infinitely worse than the plasticized, pre-packaged donor blood. So, as long as they take the potion every twenty-four hours, they're safe.

Between my job, the time spent in the archives, and the fact that I must power down most days between the hours of sunrise and sunset, there isn't much opportunity for mayhem.

There is a cure for my situation somewhere in the bowels of that building, I know it.

And one of these days, I intend to find it.

ABOUT THE AUTHOR

Elise Abram is high school teacher of English and Computer Studies, former archaeologist, editor, publisher, award winning author, avid reader of literary and science fiction, and student of the human condition. Everything she does, watches, reads and hears is fodder for her writing. She is passionate about her morning lattes, writing and language, cooking, and differentiated instruction. In her spare time, she experiments with paleo cookery, knits badly, and writes. She also bakes. Most of the time it doesn't burn. Her family doesn't seem to mind.

http://eliseabram.com

THE REVENANT
A YA PARANORMAL THRILLER WITH ZOMBIES

Raised from the dead as a revenant more than a hundred years ago, Zulu possesses superior stealth, superhuman speed, and a keen intellect. His only companion is Morgan the Seer, an old man cursed with longevity and the ability to see the future in his dreams. Zulu has spent the last century working with Morgan in order to save the people in his nightmares from horrible fates. Branded a vigilante by the media, Zulu must live his life in the shadows, travelling by night or in the city's underground, unless his quest demands otherwise.

Morgan also has enemies. His twin brother Malchus, a powerful necromancer, is raising an army of undead minions to hunt Morgan down.

Will they be able to stop Morgan from raising his army? How will they kill someone as powerful as Malchus? Is there more at stake than just their own lives?

CARRINGTON PULITZER
THE REVELATION CHRONICLES ONLINE
EXTENDED PLAYPACK

Everyone's playing the Carrington Pulitzer Revelation Chronicles Online Extended Playpack, including Bethany Wallace. No sooner has she beat the game than CSIS Agents Quinto and Nimoy show up on her doorstep (because that's not fishy). Their offer: serve her government by finding stolen and hidden secrets in the game.

When Bethany accepts, she's plunged into a Matrix-like, virtual reality. Aided by friends Cole, Glen, Tariq, and Denis, she navigates the world plagued by ginormous spiders, zombies, and jellyfishnados. When some of her friends are killed only to show up later in the game in different roles, Bethany realizes she's not just in any old video game—she's in a Carrington Pulitzer video game.

**And she's playing the part of her hero,
Carrington Pulitzer!**

Bethany and her remaining friends continue on their quest to find the missing documents, but when Bethany dies and wakes up in a strange hospital room, she learns there's more to her adventure than the CSIS agents have let on.

Through it all, Bethany is left asking the only question that will help her survive her ordeal:

What would Carrington Pulitzer do?

I WAS, AM, WILL BE ALICE

For readers of TIME TRAVELER'S WIFE and
ALICE IN WONDERLAND

Winner of the
2017 Kindle Book Review Award for Young Adult Fiction
and the
2015 A Woman's Write Competition for Fiction

When Alice Carroll is in grade three she narrowly escapes losing her life in a school shooting. All she remembers is the woman comforting her in the moments before the gunshot, and that one second she was there, the next she wasn't.

It's bad enough coming to terms with surviving while others, including her favourite teacher, didn't, let alone dealing with the fact she might wink out of existence at any time.

Alice spends the next few years seeing specialists about her Post Traumatic Stress as a result of VD—Voldemort Day—but it's not until she has a nightmare about The Day That Shall Not Be Mentioned, disappears from her bed, is found by police, and taken home to meet her four-year-old self that she realizes she's been time travelling.

Alice is unsure if her getting unstuck in time should be considered an ability or a liability, until she disappears right in front of her high school at dismissal time, the busiest time of day. Worried that someone may find out about her problem before long, Alice enlists her best friend (and maybe boyfriend), Pete, to help her try to control her shifting through time with limited success. She's just about ready to give up when the shooter is caught. Alice resolves to take control of her time travelling in order to go back to That Day, stop the shooting, and figure out the identity of the stranger who'd shielded Alice's body with her own.